BOBBY'S GIRL

A NOVEL BY ROCHELLE RATNER

BOBBY'S GIRL

COFFEE HOUSE PRESS : : MINNEAPOLIS : : 1986

The publishers thank the National Endowment for the Arts, a federal agency, for a Small Press Assistance Grant that aided in the production of this book.

Cover by Susan Nees
Back cover photo by Rhoda Sidney

Coffee House Press books are available to bookstores and libraries through our primary distributor: Consortium Book Sales & Distribution, 213 East Fourth Street, Saint Paul, Minnesota 55101. Our books are also available through most other small press distributors, and through all major library jobbers. For personal orders, catalogs or other information, write to: Coffee House Press, Box 10870, Minneapolis, MN 55440.

Library of Congress Cataloging-in-Publication Data

Ratner, Rochelle.
Bobby's girl.

Summary: Growing up in Atlantic City in the 1950s and 1960s, trapped in a suffocating family and suffering the agonies of being unpopular, the protagonist lives in a fantasy world peopled with figures from pop culture, until she finally gains the strength to face her life realistically.
[1. Emotional problems – Fiction. 2. Self-acceptance – Fiction. 3. Popularity – Fiction. 4. Atlantic City (N.J.) – Fiction] I. Title.
PS3568.A76B63 1986 813'.54 [Fic] 86-20794
ISBN 0-918273-22-6 (pbk. : alk. paper)

For Paul Pines
Without whose faith and support
this book wouldn't have happened

BOBBY'S GIRL

When people ask of me,
What would you like to be,
Now that you're not a kid
Any more,

I know just what to say,
I answer right away,
There's just one thing
I've been wishing for:

I want to be Bobby's girl,
I want to be Bobby's girl.
That's the most important thing
To me…

—Marcie Blaine

CHAPTER ONE

1959
Age ten

Songs in the Top Forty included
VENUS
LONELY BOY
POOR LITTLE FOOL
MACK THE KNIFE
DREAM LOVER
ONLY SIXTEEN

ANNETTE FUNICELLO, WHO used to be on the *Mickey Mouse Club* and then went out on her own as a singer, was her best friend. Shelley Fabares, who played Mary, the daughter on *The Donna Reed Show*, was her second-best friend. The three of them were all but inseparable when they were in California at the same time, though that happened rarely.

Frankie Avalon and Fabian were the men she was closest to, because Bob Marcucci and Pete DeAngelis managed all three of them. She and Frankie had more or less dated at times. Fabe was really too young for her. But Bobby Rydell was the man she dated mostly, when their schedules permitted it. Then there was Paul Anka, who mostly dated Annette.

Her parents' living-room/dining-room combination was maybe thirty feet wide by twenty feet long, not a bad shape for pacing. She had to pace to keep her show-biz friends with her. Otherwise they left the way real kids did, and she was alone again. She paced counterclockwise, a big circle in front of the sofa and behind the coffee table, around the dining-room table, past the kitchen door, and back again. Every so often she briefly reversed the circle, so as not to get dizzy. The dachshund entered after the first ten minutes or so and crouched safely underneath the dining-room table where he wouldn't get stepped on, his body stretched out long, neck and chin on the floor, eyes wide open, watching, his left ear tossed back over his head and inside out in a gesture of I-don't-care. *She* was the one who didn't care. Sometimes her father pointed to the dog and told her the dog was confused, that she was making her dog crazy and he was going to turn vicious on account of her. This could go on for hours. She could wear a track in the carpet, as her father accused her of doing. Her body rocked slightly. Pacing helped her focus.

Annette Funicello and Shelley Fabares both lived with their parents. She envied them because their parents went along with their careers and encouraged them. She thought it was funny, when she stopped to think about it, that Bobby, Paul, Frankie, even Fabe—all the boys—had moved out on their own, just as she had. Her managers, Bob Marcucci and Pete DeAngelis, especially Bob, were like substitute parents. She sometimes dared them by purposely acting up, and Bob sometimes had to take a firm hand with her. She pretended to be how old? Seventeen. Sometimes eighteen or nineteen, depending. Just so long as she was over ten, past this awful time she was going through now. It was good having Fabe and Frankie going through the same scenes with Bob and Pete. They were like her brothers and consoled her.

Take last night, for instance. She had a TV show to do next weekend, and Bob told her to go home and get to bed early. Then Bobby called, and she went out with him. Usually no one found out, but people were starting to know her around town. Dick Clark, who was supposed to be her friend, ran into them and might well have told on her. She woke up scared this morning.

She called Frankie and asked him if he'd drive into the office with her, just in case. It wasn't all that unusual. It was expensive to park downtown, and they frequently drove in together.

"Bobby's in town, by the way." She strained to make her voice sound casual. At times like that, all the acting lessons in the world didn't seem to help much. "He came over last night, and we went out for a while, did the gallery tour."

"I thought Bob wanted you to get to bed early."

"Yeah, well..." Oh Christ, Frankie was slipping into his big-brother know-it-all role again. All of twenty-one, the hot shot.

"Look," he said. "You know you have to look good for the show. It's stupid to overdo things."

"We ran into Dick in Molly Barnes' Gallery." She said it softly, her voice rising at the end, almost to a question.

"That was smart. Why the hell did you go where people might see you? Haven't you at least learned that much by now? And I'll bet you stayed up half the night worrying, too. Jesus."

Silence. Frankie looked straight ahead at the traffic. Two full stoplights before he turned to her. "Dick won't tell," he said with that smile she loved so much. Now he knew why she called him this morning. His whole scolding game was just something to pass the time in traffic.

And, anyway, it turned out Bob didn't know this time.

Her father tiptoed into the kitchen for a glass of milk. She could feel him staring at her. He was as sad and confused as he claimed the dachshund was, but with his bushy black mustache, too large for his small face, he looked more like a chipmunk. He was nearing sixty, exhausted from a twelve-hour day at work, too old for children. His thick, black-framed reading glasses were pushed up on his forehead, as if he didn't have the energy to take them off completely. His feet were popping out of his backless slippers.

Not now, please not now – they were all in Bob's office, joking, really being friends, carefree. She was almost tempted to confess she went out last night. Bob knew in the end that kids needed their fun, needed to be somewhat reckless. That was why she loved him.

Then the blow came. "The news is almost on," her father said. Silence. "They're broadcasting parts of Castro's speech today. You ought to hear it. You ought to find out what's happening in the world. You might realize there are people with larger problems than you have. Real problems, not imaginary ones."

She reversed the circle to avoid walking past him. He stood there, fidgeting, his eyes blinking from the strain of watching her. A louder silence.

He walked quickly back to the den, turned the television up a little louder, so he wouldn't have to think about her. Either that or he was getting hard of hearing, but he would never admit that. She slowed down her pace. Her thoughts were starting to wander. What would it have been like if she had brothers and sisters, a real family? Maybe she wouldn't have needed to pace, if she'd had real friends, at least. This sort of thought led nowhere and broke into the fantasy. It was her father's fault. Damn him. She stooped to fix the dog's ear and felt his body tighten up, his long backbone coiling away from her ever so slightly. He couldn't make up his mind. She petted him, spoke softly, took some sleeping pills – two Tuinol and a couple of Valium – and went into her room and closed the door. Peace and quiet.

𝄞 Actually the circle used to be a straight line. The pacing used to have a purpose. It used to lead somewhere, to school, Union Avenue School, ten blocks from home, blocks in alphabetical order: Kenyon, Lancaster, Manchester, Nassau, Osborne, Pembroke, Quincy, Rumson, Swarthmore, Thurlow, Union. Her whole life ordered. Annette, Shelley, Frankie, Fabe – they were her friends for the walk at least, out in the open air where they could breathe. They didn't forget her the way Arlene had back in first grade. Arlene was the daughter of her mother's best friend and was supposed to walk her home at lunchtime. One day Arlene got talking with her friends and just left her standing there.

Ever since that day, she'd had her own friends on the walk home. She had her friends to console her two years ago, when she was eight years old and Rebel, her beagle puppy, was run over by a dump truck on Jerome Avenue. Even Harriet, her grown-up next-door neighbor, who would have understood how she felt, wasn't at home. Rebel had dug his way out of the pen her father had built for him.

Of course, as she aged, her circle of friends had grown. There were fights, and there were people who didn't like each other, just as in life, but in the end they were all her friends, and they always forgave her. That was what real friendship was.

Shelley Fabares and Annette Funicello were both tutored on the sets when they were working. Fabe went to public schools in Philadelphia a good part of the year. His parents insisted that he not be singled out. Paul, Frankie, and Bobby had all graduated, though they talked of going to college someday. But, for her, there never seemed to be a question of studying. She simply avoided that.

She turned the music louder, the way her father turned up the TV or her mother raised her voice talking on the phone when she could hear her daughter's footsteps pacing the next room. All that thought of school was starting to upset her. She tried hard to focus on the words of one song after another:

Venus, if you will,
Please send a little
Girl for me to thrill,
A girl who wants my
Kisses and my arms,
A girl with all the charms
Of you.

Probably the other kids had stereos. She was seldom in their houses long enough to find out, and when she was, she found herself too nervous to look around. Arlene had a Victrola, with a black plastic case and a long thick thimble that you piled the forty-fives on and let them drop one after another. She knew she didn't want that, didn't want anything Arlene had.

She remembered the small record player she had as a little girl, with decals on its lid of Mary and her little lamb. She loved to put the records on one by one, playing games like "I choose you because you're yellow" or "I choose you because you've been sitting there so patiently." Half the fun was playing them one by one. So she convinced her parents to buy her the best manual record player they could find, but it was still, they told her, a glorified child's toy, since, they told her, everyone with any sense bought the other kind, like Arlene's.

Records were also a problem. Her parents had one or two cha-cha records that they played when they practiced steps from their dance class. They took lessons from the same teacher they later sent her to. Watching them dance so awkwardly on her pacing carpet, with her father stepping on her mother's feet, anyone would have thought they'd learn that dancing couldn't be taught. But they didn't seem to notice.

"My Son the Folk Singer," by Allan Sherman, was another record her parents owned, but you didn't have to dance to it. She enjoyed that. And about once a month, when her parents went shopping at Garwood Mills, the first discount store in Atlantic City, she prevailed upon them to let her buy a forty-five, and she got "It's Only Make Believe" by Conway Twitty, "Diana" by Paul Anka, "All I Have to Do Is Dream" by the Everly Brothers, and Frankie's recording of "Venus." She also had a record by Marty DeNico, the South Philly teenager Uncle Steve managed. He'd actually grown up with Fabe, Frankie, and Bobby, and the record was a demo that said NOT FOR SALE on its label: her most treasured possession.

For her tenth-birthday present, her parents said she could choose any album she wanted. She went up to Garwood Mills alone and stared and stared, with nobody rushing her this time. She looked at the album covers, picked up a few to read the backs, but most of the companies were smart enough to put the important notes inside so you had to buy the record if you wanted to read them. At last she chose an album by Fabian, his first. It had a bright orange cover with the face of the handsome thirteen-year-old staring almost shyly at her. It was a false double album: only one record. Inside, the cover promised more color photos, a pull-out portrait suitable for framing, plus the liner notes. She read, for the first time, how Fabe was discovered sitting on a stoop in South Philly after his father had just been taken to the hospital with a heart attack. Fabe agreed to sing only because he knew it was up to him to look after the family now. It said his father was a policeman: Dominic Forte. She already knew that Bob Marcucci and Pete DeAngelis owned Chancellor Records, which produced the album. She did what little she could to help support them.

She held the pull-out portrait in her hands. For a moment she thought of just tacking it up on the wall over her bed, where maybe she would dream of him. But she never remembered her dreams anyway, only the nightmares. Besides, she had something better than dreams and much more private. To tack it up on the wall would cheapen it. That was what the other kids did. She imagined pinups all over their rooms, the girls talking about new records in voices as shrill as her mother's. Gossip, that's what it was. She wanted no part of it. She put the portrait back in the album and tucked the album away in a drawer where even the maid wouldn't find it. No one must know of this.

When she was little, she didn't have to hide her games and fantasies. People used to marvel at how creative she was. Her mother used to tell her she'd grow up to be an artist and called her "my little artist" so often that she cringed when she heard the words. One of her favorite games was played with marbles. She'd take out the big cardboard Chinese-checkers board her mother had gotten from the abandoned playground. She'd dump her cans of marbles on the floor – thousands of them. She'd call this star eighth grade, this star seventh grade, this star sixth grade, and so on. She'd begin with eighth grade and choose the prettiest marbles first, the way they did in kickball, until all the stars were filled. The big shooter marbles would be the teachers. Some marbles were always left out, and they were always the same ones. She never chose them.

𝄞 Every time her mother's parents came to visit, they carried presents. Sometimes Grandpa Jess and Grandma Shirley brought coloring books, sometimes games or an outfit for her doll, and one time they brought sewing cards. The presents she liked best came in boxes. She would undo the wrapping and fold it carefully, the way her mother had told her, so they would be able to use it again. She would open the box and thank them for it, but she never let her mother throw the box away. The whole next week she would keep it in her room, taking it out, wrapping it up again, giving herself a present.

Then her mother taught her how to make dolls out of different-sized boxes, tying the boxes together, the largest one for the torso, long thin ones for the arms and legs, and a square box for the head, and then covering it all with crepe paper. "You're building a sculpture," her mother had said. "That's one of the best mannequins I've ever seen. Not many girls your age could build something that good. I love that you chose turquoise paper to cover him. It shows how imaginative you are. Most kids would make his skin pink or beige." She had chosen turquoise because she remembered the turquoise stuffed poodle offered as one of the prizes at the Million Dollar Pier. Her parents were never able to win it for her, so this was the next-best thing. She believed her mother really liked the turquoise doll until she realized that praise was another way of calling her an artist.

𝄞 It happened once and could someday happen again. She was at Auntie Sue's when Uncle Norman, who wasn't really her uncle just as Auntie Sue wasn't really her aunt, came home from a business trip. Arlene and Richard ran to meet him at the door. He was a big man, but he still couldn't carry all the presents he had brought them. Arlene and Richard tore the wrappings off, barely thanking him for one before opening the next. There were two new Barbie dolls and a lot of different outfits for them: skating clothes, hiking clothes, a great gold swimsuit. Arlene got a new beaded sweater. Arlene loved clothes. She let her parents dress her up in all those horrible, delicate things and let her mother fuss with her mustard-colored hair. Then she'd just sit there with her dress all smoothed out, smiling. Arlene could spend hours dressing some stupid doll. Richard opened a Clue game, a junior chemistry set, binoculars that folded up to put in your pocket, and cowboys and horses, large ones with ten-gallon hats and removable saddles and stirrups and boots with spurs and fingers that could bend around the reins.

She sat there. Her mother sat there. Even Auntie Sue sat there. They weren't given anything. Finally Auntie Sue called Richard aside. He went up to his room and came down again with a small white horse and cowboy.

"You were playing with this earlier," he said, holding it out to her. "You can take him home if you want."

"Do you mean it?"

"Sure."

"You won't ask for him back?"

"No, I promise. I don't really need it now anyway." He glanced over at the two new ones sitting on the table. "I know you'll take good care of it."

She *would* take good care of it, she promised. She felt included for the first time in what seemed like hours. But she also knew Auntie Sue had asked him to give her something, and she felt bad about that. Bad for him, too. She wouldn't have wanted to give up any of her toys, regardless how many she had. Besides, it didn't even have a box with it.

𝄞 Richard was the closest thing she had to a family. When she was two or three, her parents told her, he was so entranced with her that he'd follow her around, imitating all her actions, making sure she didn't fall, looking after her. But that stopped when she got older.

She was ten. Richard was thirteen or fourteen, in his first year of high school. His parents went to Florida for two weeks and took Arlene with them. Richard couldn't afford to miss that much school, so he stayed at her house. He brought their telephone over and plugged it into the extra jack, hoping it would ring when someone dialed his number. It didn't.

Only she and her mother were home with him. There must have been a fight about something. Richard ran into the kitchen and grabbed a butcher knife. He ran back to the guest room, no longer screaming, just flashing that knife blade up near his throat. He slammed the door.

Her mother was hysterical, pounding on the door. "Open up, Richie, please."

"Leave me alone."

"Richie, open up. I'm sorry." Then, under her breath: "Where'd I put the key? It must be here somewhere."

"Open the door and I'll kill myself."

"Richie, please come out. I'm sorry. I didn't mean to yell at you."

"Don't come in here. Don't come near me. Open that door and I'll cut my throat."

"Richie, please. I'll give you money for the movies. Just come out. Please. Please."

Silence. Then her mother pleading again. Then more silence. She listened from behind the closed door of her own room. Tears, more pleading, then the sound of the door opening. Richie walked calmly, firmly toward the kitchen.

Once in a while Grandma Dora, her father's mother, the grandma she really loved, babysat on Sunday night at her house. She liked that more than anything except those times when she stayed at Grandma Dora's and they slept together in the big double bed. Grandma Dora was as lonely as she was, and they played games together and shared things. Her bedtime was eight o'clock, only Grandma Dora let her stay up till nine on account of Ed Sullivan. She remembered how the dancers fanned in and out of their circle and how the camera always panned them from above. Or was that Jackie Gleason? Anyway, they were girls in tutus. Sometimes Arlene said she wanted to grow up to be one of them.

Then one night Ed Sullivan did something strange. Mostly his guests were singers like Frank Sinatra or Enzo Stuarti, musicians like Liberace, or comedians like Jerry Lewis. But this time he had a guy with long hair and a guitar, and he couldn't sing—just sort of shouted. Elvis Pretzel, her father called him. Her mother called him Elvis Pelvis. Grandma Dora made her go to bed at eight now.

𝄞 She was in fifth grade, and she was on the safety patrol—not the guides, who wore arm bands and led the younger kids into classes, but the patrol, who wore large belts strapped across their chests and even in the pouring rain stood out on street corners and helped kids cross the streets before and after school. Jeanie and Jill were the captain and lieutenant: tall, thin Jeanie and short, cocky Jill. They were like Mutt and Jeff in the comic strip. Only it wasn't funny. Jeanie and Jill always used to pick on her. They were in the older class.

Anyway, trouble was brewing. The teacher in charge of the safeties was too strict with her classes. All the safeties were going to resign in protest at the meeting after school that Friday. She even told her mother about it.

On Friday afternoon, she led the kids across the street for fifteen minutes and then went back to school, to the meeting. She planned to walk out with the other kids or stay if they stayed. It felt good to be included, whatever happened. But

Miss Tandem met her at the classroom door and blocked her way. She let the other kids in and then stepped out in the hall to talk with her. The giant figure backed her up against the wall. "I've had some bad reports about you," she said.

"What?"

"I've heard you're not stepping out into the street to look both ways before you let the children cross."

"But I do. Honest I do."

"That's not what I've been hearing."

Silence.

"I think you might be a little too young to be on the safeties."

She thought she was blacking out. She heard Miss Tandem asking, for the second time, if she could please have her badge back.

The group walkout never happened, but that wasn't what she told her mother. The reports to Miss Tandem had been from Jeanie and Jill, of course, the same Jeanie and Jill with whom, six months later, she would be forced to go to dancing school.

CHAPTER TWO

1962
Age thirteen

Songs in the Top Forty included
JOHNNY ANGEL
ROSES ARE RED
RETURN TO SENDER
SOLDIER BOY
HE'S A REBEL

SHE SPRAWLED ON HER unmade bed paging through the latest issue of *Sixteen*. There was a photo story about a dream date with Ricky Nelson and "Twenty Things I Want My Girl to Be," by Bobby Vinton. There was the "Betty at *Bandstand*" cartoon. The old alphabet rhyme went through her head as she read the captions: "B, her name is Betty, and she has a blond ponytail, and she lives in Boston, where every day she faithfully watches *Bandstand*." In the first episode, when Betty was fifteen, her father was transferred to Philadelphia. Betty couldn't believe it, Philadelphia for real! Now she could really go to *Bandstand*.

Then Betty learned that only the regulars got in easily. Every day for three weeks, she waited in line after school. At last she got in. She had a pass for a week, though, a week at *Bandstand* — her! Maybe on camera, even. But the camera mostly focused on the dancers, and Betty was on the side, not knowing enough boys yet to have a boyfriend. It didn't matter, though. She was inside with Mike and Frani and Carmen and Freddie and all the others. At one point Carmen almost spoke to her. And after this week she would get in line again. She would get in again, over and over until boys danced with her, until one boy danced only with her, until Dick noticed how well they danced and people watching at home started looking for them on camera, and before you knew it, Dick had made them regulars. Betty kept her fingers crossed in hopes it would happen, though all along she knew in her heart that it would.

She thrust the magazine against the pillow in disgust. Idle dreams, idle childish dreams. Betty deserved the cartoonlike format in which *Sixteen* drew her. They didn't intend her to be taken seriously. Why bother with her when all around her in the magazine there were stories of the stars, of real people? You couldn't even turn on the TV and watch Betty dancing. Betty was never going to be accepted by the regulars. She knew it from the start.

Well, she certainly wasn't a Betty. It was easy enough to understand how Betty felt, though, standing by the wall and watching the others dance. Walls are cold places. How well she remembered them. In seventh grade last year it was simple. She could just decide not to go to the once-a-month Friday-night dance. She'd gone only to the first dance that year, wearing a starched nylon dress that made her whole body itch, and hoped that by some magic a boy would emerge from the wall to dance with her.

She hated the junior-high-school gym to begin with, and with all those sagging crepe-paper streamers stretched across it, streamers that were torn by nine o'clock because rowdy boys jumped up to grab them, the gym looked even worse than usual. Also, the music was too loud, and the only songs they played were the fast ones like "Peppermint Twist," "Tossin' and Turnin'," and "Pony Time." She'd spent an hour putting her hair in a French twist, and she knew if she danced it would fall out immediately. Strands were coming loose already, and they hung limp over her sweating forehead. She saw her seventh-grade teacher walking in her direction and ran out to the Coke machine before he could notice she was standing there alone. They hadn't even bothered to put chairs out. They just expected that they'd all be making fools of themselves dancing.

It was like waiting around to be picked for kickball. A girl didn't put herself on a team, even when it got down to the end. She had to wait till they chose her, saying all the while under her breath that she wouldn't fumble, not this time. But the first ball got past her and rolled all the way to the fence, because she was afraid and backed away instead of rushing toward it. Always she backed away, the second time even farther, because she was ashamed by then.

It was as bad as that awful six weeks away at camp two summers ago. She had no escape then. Her bunk was privileged enough to go to the dance, and the counselors insisted she had to go with them. She tried to find the safest wall, one where the other outcasts weren't gathered, so that at least she didn't have to associate herself with them.

Stacy was there with her. Stacy, a girl as short as she, had her brown hair cut in a pixie just like hers. She liked Stacy, and the two of them stood together. One of the Bunk Six boys, a popular boy who was dancing with Arlene, led another boy over to them. He wanted to dance with someone, and Arlene must have told him they were good prospects. She and Stacy stood flat against the wall, trying to make themselves taller, staring ahead, blank-eyed. She wished she had learned how to smile the way other girls did. The boy thought for a moment.

Then, pointing his finger, he went eenie-meenie-miney-mo. It landed on her. He walked off with Stacy. She had the corner all to herself now, as if she had done something wrong and had been forced to stand there. Stacy was ecstatic.

Stacy was crying. It was a week later – or maybe only a day or two later, time was moving so slowly. Stacy had been out with Jim. She came into the cabin and threw herself down on the cot in tears. Arlene, Judy, and all the other popular girls ran over to comfort her. When the crowd was breaking up, when most of the others had gone back to their Monopoly or jacks games, she cautiously approached Stacy.

"What's wrong, Stace? Can I help with anything?"

Stacy didn't even look up at her.

"Does it have to do with Jim?" she ventured. "Did he say something that upset you?" She listened to Stacy sucking in, swallowing the mucus running in her nose. "Hey, he's not worth it. Really, he's not. No boy is." She moved a step closer.

Stacy lifted her head and looked at her for a second. "Oh, how do you know? You wouldn't understand anything." Then she went back to crying harder than ever. They never shared their corners after that.

𝄞 "Hurry up," she cried, yanking Annette into the ladies' room behind her. "You're not going to believe this." She checked to make sure there was nobody else around and dragged Annette into a far corner.

"This better be good," Annette said. "I felt like an idiot running off with you and leaving everyone sitting there." Annette was still nervous around Bob and Pete. She'd barely known them before last year, when she started making beach-party flicks with Frankie.

"It's good, I promise. Look." She held out the small gold

chain. "Bobby gave it to me this afternoon. It's a Saint Christopher medal, and it used to belong to his grandmother." Annette rubbed her fingers over it tenderly. *Gina Ridarelli* was engraved on the back. "Bobby was worried about me going on the road next week. He said he wanted me to have it."

"It's gorgeous," Annette said. "Put it on."

"I don't dare. Bob would have a fit if he found out. He insists the fans still want to think I'm fifteen, and he doesn't seem to have realized yet that even at fifteen a lot of girls go steady."

"Speaking of Bob, hadn't we better get back out there before he gets suspicious?" Annette applied fresh lipstick and dabbed at her lips with a tissue, to make it look as if she'd really spent time freshening up. Not that she needed it. Even on the set, she could go for hours without having to redo her makeup. As a final touch, she held her hands to her head and made mouse ears with her fingers. The two girls burst out laughing. "We'd better get back," Annette said again.

"I guess so." She didn't agree, but Annette's nervousness was starting to bother her.

"God, I don't know what I'd have done if you hadn't been meeting us tonight. I simply had to tell you."

"I'm going to absolutely die after the movie's finished," Annette said. "I haven't had so much fun since the *Mickey Mouse Club*."

"I guess you'll just have to keep making beach-party movies for the rest of your life," she teased. They had gotten a lot of good laughs out of how superficial those movies were. She was still a little disappointed that Bob had forbidden her to accept the part after it was offered to her. He was worried about her being too closely associated with Frankie. But having her best friend playing Dee Dee was almost as good.

"You're so lucky," Annette whispered, as they were walking back to the table. "Paul's written songs like 'Puppy Love' for me and all, but he's never given me a secret token of his affection or anything like that."

Even back at the table, working hard to make normal conversation with Bob, Pete, and Frankie, she felt like the luckiest girl in the world.

𝄞 They referred to it afterward as the day the record stuck. Then they'd laugh about it. It became like one of those anecdotes parents tell about their children, some incident from when the kid was four or five. In the telling, the stranger is let in on the secret and accepted into the family – an endearment, the kind of anecdote her parents were ashamed to tell.

They'd be sitting there talking, say at a dinner party, with ten or twelve people, a few of whom she was really close to, Fabe or Frankie maybe. Whenever Dick Clark was around, sooner or later the subject would turn to *Bandstand*. And sooner or later Dick would say, "Did we ever tell you about the day the record stuck?"

She would blush a bit. It was expected of her. And there would be laughter, gentle, feminine, childlike.

Dick would explain, if the others didn't already know, how on *Bandstand* the singers always lip-synched to their records because the show didn't have an orchestra. "What was it, your third appearance on the show?" he would ask her.

"Second," she'd answer, gratified that by this little slip he'd shown that he looked back as if he knew her better than he did at the time. "I was singing 'Learning to Love.'" She was giggling already. The old nervousness came back just in thinking about it.

"It was around the middle of the song," Dick continued. "How's that go – 'I can learn to hold you tight, I can learn to kiss good-night...'"

She sang the words. "The record stuck on the second 'I can learn.' I realized what happened right away, but I tried to cover it. I didn't know when or *if* the engineer would pick it up, so I had to fall a second behind. I sang it about five times. Then I couldn't control myself any longer and burst out laughing."

"We all did," Dick added, then, turning to her: "Actually, I have a feeling the engineer picked it up sooner but decided to let it go and see what would happen. Tony's capable of that."

"You never told me that!" she half-shrieked, somewhat playfully angry. Well, he *hadn't* mentioned that before.

Dick was beaming like a naughty six-year-old. She was tempted to throw a potato at him, but she controlled herself and beamed back instead. That day had been special. She had proven herself adaptable to the situation. She'd proved she could laugh at herself. She'd won his love, just like Frankie, Fabe, Bobby, all the kids he'd watched grow up. From that day on, she'd been one of the family. It was the kind of thing another girl in her place might have written home about.

𝄞 She wanted to be like other kids, so she watched the kids dancing. She listened to the chosen few talk about their lives, hanging onto every word. She listened to Dick's lead-ins to the commercials in which the boys' and girls' faces changed in just one week from all broken out to smooth and kissable. She didn't really want to be kissed, but she was supposed to. Day after day, week after week, she watched the same faces and memorized the words, till at last she found a pimple on her forehead.

She went to the drugstore two blocks away, on Ventnor and Lancaster avenues, where the druggist knew her and knew her mother but still sold her cigarettes once. When she had a virus years ago, this same druggist gave her mother samples of an orange, candy-coated pill she learned to swallow to avoid the horrid taste of the medicine. From him she bought the Clearasil.

Alone in the house, in the bathroom, she opened the pink and beige plastic tube, squeezed a bit onto her finger, a shade lighter than her skin, and rubbed it over the pimple. Then she squeezed another drop for the area to the left of the pimple and a third drop for the area to the right. Only it didn't seem enough, so she went over the whole area again. She would follow this ritual for a week, and in a week her face would be not only clear and soft but as attractive as the face on television.

She slept on it. The next morning there were two pimples. She had gotten the Clearasil just in time. She spread it on again, slowly, heavily, every morning and night, faithfully. Dick would be proud of her. In a week the tube was almost empty, and her face was a large mass of pimples, half of them infected. It was the only time in her life that her skin broke out.

𝄞 Like the other girls in the freshman class, she wore knee socks held up by rubber bands under the folded tops. They cut off the circulation in her legs, while Frankie, Bobby, even Pat Boone sang of girls in bobbysocks. They would have been so much easier to wear. Even the girls on *Bandstand* didn't care if they slid down at their ankles.

On Saturdays she spent hours in the five-and-ten-cent stores looking for knee socks to match the colors of her plaid skirts: magenta for the magenta and green plaid, gold for the black and gold plaid. She always picked the brightest color, but they somehow looked drab after she'd worn them once or twice. Her big toes would poke holes through them. But anything, anything was preferable to those stockings she knew would rip the second she put them on or would get holes from her bitten fingernails, those stockings Frankie sang about, worn by a girl ready for love.

𝄞 Uncle Steve got her and her friend Donna into the Steel Pier for free. That proved he had the right connections. He'd tried—for two days he'd called backstage, so they could maybe meet Paul Anka. But Paul wouldn't answer, or was on stage, or back at the room resting.

"Do you know Steve Carter?" she asked, stretching her arm out in a sea of waving arms. Paul nodded quizzically and stared at a girl on the other side, who was a lot prettier.

"Hey, Steve says hello," she called.

"Yeah, tell him hi for me," Paul said, handing her an autographed picture.

Big shot. Too damn concerned with himself, Paul Anka the famous singer, forgetting the friends who helped him to the top. Uncle Steve said most of them forgot. They always seemed to forget him.

She decided then and there that she didn't like Paul Anka, and that was one of the reasons he dated Annette and not her. They had a sort of sparring friendship. He was always a bit cocky, a lot like her. But he was a good singer.

For the first three shows, she and Donna sat in the front, in the seats you paid for, and waved their arms frantically when Paul asked for a girl to come up from the audience. Then they realized he needed a girl with blue eyes or the song wouldn't rhyme right.

Uncle Steve was almost, but never quite, there when she needed him. He was a tease. A few weeks before, he said he tried to call her, to go to Wildwood with him to see Ike and Tina Turner, but she wasn't home. He said Bobby Rydell was there with his parents. They came late, and if it hadn't been for Steve, they might not have gotten in. They joined him at his table. Unlike Paul, Bobby never forgot those who helped him.

"Next time," Uncle Steve said, he'd take her with him.

That was a magic summer. She stayed at Grandma Dora's, behind the A&P in the brick duplex with its own little garden out back. She said it was closer to where Donna was staying on her summer visit from Philadelphia. Since they were together so much, it made things easier. But really she stayed there to be close to Uncle Steve, to be close to his stories, in hopes he would take her along next time, next time.

Grandma Dora never hit the five-foot mark. Her bright blue eyes always seemed to look up, wide open, vulnerable. Tim Katzman took advantage of Grandma Dora's good-heartedness. Tim played drums behind Eddie Fisher, and Uncle Steve had been Eddie Fisher's friend since way back when. Eddie kept offering Steve a job as road manager, which he never took because he didn't want to leave Grandma Dora alone. That summer there was a mix-up at the hotel. There wasn't enough room for the whole band, and Uncle Steve brought Tim home with him. Tim was like a son. He told Grandma Dora stories about his mother. He wanted homemade potato latkes, and she didn't have the strength to chop potatoes, so he chopped them for her.

Tim was a substitute uncle. Only he came through. Not only did he take her and Grandma Dora to see the show, but he took them backstage afterward, to meet Eddie. Upstairs, rather. The image was embedded in her mind: Grandma Dora holding onto the rail, trying her best to take it step by step. But the stairs were too much for her. When they entered Eddie's dressing room, her face was red, and she was out of breath. She said she had to take a pill. Eddie had no idea who she was and saw only that she was with Tim – no, with Steve, Uncle Steve. He ran to get her some water.

"No. No, thank you," she stuttered. She pointed to her

mouth, to her tongue. This pill was not taken with water but placed under the tongue. "It's nitroglycerin," she said when it was almost dissolved and she was able to talk better.

Eddie stood there confused, still holding the glass of water. Finally he set it on the table and sat down next to her, silent, his hand resting on hers, like the doctor's hand when he took her blood pressure – calming and reassuring. "So you're Steve's mother," he said at last. "Steve's spoken a lot about you."

She sat there beaming, silent.

"You live in Atlantic City all year round, don't you?"

"Yes. Steve was born here. Both my boys were born here."

"I've always wondered what it's like here in the winter."

"It's quiet. A few big conventions. Being right on the ocean means there's not a lot of snow."

Eddie's eyes searched the room, as if for a clue as to what to say next. He focused on Tim. "It's really wonderful of you to let Tim stay with you. I still don't know what happened with our reservations."

She kept beaming.

"My grandmother really loves having him there. He's like another son to her." This was the first time the little girl had spoken.

"Let's see, you're Steve's daughter?"

"Niece." She said it with a certain pride: he doesn't have to include me. He does it because he really wants to.

He asked if they'd enjoyed the show.

"Yes," they said in unison.

She tried to think of a song to single out as a special favorite, but she couldn't remember any. All she could think of was what was happening right now. They were up in Eddie's dressing room, and he was talking to them, just to them.

At last Steve came over. "We should be getting home," he said.

As they stood up to leave, Eddie bent down and kissed Grandma Dora, once on each cheek. "You take care of yourself now," he said. "Don't try any more stairs like that."

All their lives they would love Eddie for coming through like that.

Meanwhile, they never heard from Tim again.

Four years later, when Grandma Dora was dying, she got everything confused. She insisted she had to get to her niece's wedding, and Grandma Dora seemed to think that *she* was the one getting married – and marrying Tim. That was the last time Grandma Dora went out of the nursing home. She died happy even though Tim was never there. What went on in the mind was what really mattered.

She went with Frankie, Fabe, Bob, and Pete to see Eddie's show, and like all entertainers they were invited backstage afterward. She was the only one who had met him before. She walked over and hugged him as soon as their eyes met.

"I don't know if you'll remember me, but I met you years ago. Steve Carter's my uncle. My grandmother and I met you after one of your shows at the Five Hundred Club in Atlantic City."

"Of course I remember."

"My grandmother was sick, and you got her water to take a pill. I'll never forget that."

"Only she didn't need water to take the pill," Eddie laughed. "I must have looked awfully silly standing there holding it."

"You looked wonderful."

"How's your grandmother feeling now?"

"She died a few years ago."

"I'm sorry to hear that."

"There's no need to be. You provided an incredible memory. Even when she was really sick, she never forgot that night."

"I haven't seen Steve in years. What's he doing now?"

"Still selling liquor. He's been seeing a lovely woman, and that takes up a good deal of his time."

"Please give him my best when you speak to him. Steve's one of the finest people I ever met. He was always doing things for other people, like taking Tim home with him. A really good guy."

She beamed like Grandma Dora. All this was important to her, since Steve was the only member of the family she had kept in touch with. She wished like hell she could get him to be her road manager or could find some other spot for him in her organization, but really Bob and Pete were all she needed, and Uncle Steve said he didn't want to leave town anyway.

When they left the restaurant, where they'd gone after the club, Bob mentioned that Eddie never forgot the people who'd helped him get his start. He said he expected all of them to act the same, as if she'd ever needed to be told that.

Donna was like everyone else. She forgot the people who'd been good to her. She went back to Philadelphia after that summer, and she never called, never wrote. Donna had simply been using her because she didn't know any other kids in Atlantic City. That summer, thanks to Donna, she had given up all her other friends. When she went back to school in September, they had made new friends, and no one seemed to have time for her. That pushed her over the edge, drew her into the fantasy almost completely.

Donna was being her friend only because their parents were close and she had nothing better to do. The days were so boring, they even sat and watched the horse dive. They screamed through five Paul Anka shows, six Frankie Avalons, five Fabians, and eight Bobby Rydells. They went to hear Ricky Nelson and Bobby Vinton. But Donna was only faking excitement. If she liked those shows so much, how come she'd never, not even once, gone to *Bandstand*? She was living right there in Philadelphia, right in Center City. What was wrong with her? Donna would turn eighteen next May. She had only another six months before she'd be over the age limit.

"Oh, we're not allowed to go there," Donna told her. It was one of those nights when she'd brought Donna home to sleep over at her parents' house. "I go to a private school, don't forget. They're uptight. They think if we went to *Bandstand*, if people caught sight of the insignia on our uniforms, it would cheapen the school's image. A few years ago, two girls went, and they were suspended."

"So go home first and change out of your uniform. Or wear a sweater to hide the insignia, like Carmen does. They'll never know the difference."

"Maybe, but it's not worth the risk."

They turned out the light. She lay awake as Donna's breathing deepened and she drifted off to sleep. How could she be friends with such a scaredy-cat, such a goody-goody? Donna didn't have to go and dance, being overweight and all, but at least she could go hear the singers. If only *she* lived in Philadelphia, nothing would keep her away from there. Before the summer ended, she had to convince Donna to go next year, at least once.

Suddenly she felt terribly alone. Donna was no help. And even in her wildest dreams her mother couldn't help her. It was no use trying to share fantasies any more. Her mother used to tell her she dreamed she would someday marry a man who was a great dancer, and the two of them would travel all over the country winning dance contests. She dated one guy only because he could dance so well. Then she ended up marrying a man who had two left feet. That was what their daughter inherited.

 Mike wasn't able to drive yet.

For the past month she'd watched *Bandstand* every day, waiting, hoping, praying for Mike and Frani to win the twist contest. At last they won. The prize was two red Pontiac Firebird convertibles with black leather upholstery, one for each of them. Frani lived in Philly, like most of the other kids, and could drive her car home if she wanted to. Mike, it turned out, lived in New Jersey, where you had to be seventeen to drive, and he wouldn't be seventeen for another five months. Then, what with permits and tests, the car would be last year's model before he got to drive it.

She knew how much driving meant to him. New Jersey, *any* place in New Jersey, had to be a million miles away from Philly. She imagined he lived somewhere south of Cherry Hill, close to Hammonton, not far from her. Driving meant all but life or death to him.

He already knew how to drive, of course, even how to shift. His father had taught him, just as her father had taught her when she was eight or nine years old. It was something she and her father did together. He took her with him on Saturdays and let her work the floor shift in the Hilman Huskie. On those days she sat in front, close to him. Her mother, when she rode with them, was always afraid they'd hit someone. She jammed her foot against the empty floor, as if the brake were there, or folded her arms tightly across her chest, long before there were seat belts. She was just as happy to let her daughter sit in front. In the back, she could pretend not to see anything.

As soon as she turned seventeen, her father would teach her to drive again. She had only three and a half years to go. One way or another, she would get herself a car and drive off, free to go anywhere, do anything. She was exactly the opposite of her mother. She would drive away from Atlantic City and never come back. In control. This thought gave her hope for the future, her only reason to live sometimes.

CHAPTER THREE

September 1962 – March 1964
Ages thirteen to fifteen

Songs in the Top Forty included
IT'S MY PARTY
BLUE VELVET
MY BOYFRIEND'S BACK
HE'S SO FINE
WALK LIKE A MAN

In October 1962, Marcie Blaine recorded BOBBY'S GIRL.

CARLA PHONED AT ELEVEN o'clock one Friday night. She was shocked when her mother called her to the phone. No one ever called her, certainly not on Friday night, when everyone else had dates.

"Hi. Are you still up?"

"Sure."

"Marc, Arlene, and I are over at Dave's. We just got back from the movies, and we're hanging out here." Dave was Harriet's son. They lived next door, in a house like hers except that the attic had been refinished into a recreation room, the sort of room her parents claimed they couldn't afford and had no use for.

Did Carla call just to gloat about how many friends she had? That was something Arlene would do. She was so caught up in this cycle of thought that she almost didn't hear Carla.

"Why don't you come over?"

"Great. Just give me a few minutes to change." She wanted to sound as though she would put on better clothes for them, as if she changed three or four times a day, the way some girls did. She had been in her pajamas since nine-thirty. She went to bed early to avoid facing Friday night alone.

They didn't call her over just to make fun of her, the way other kids had, the way Arlene often did. Even she and Arlene were friendly now. She was close to Carla, and she'd all but grown up with Marc and Dave. If she couldn't relax with them, who could she have fun with? If only they hadn't been dancing, she would have been all right. If only Marc and not Dave had asked her to dance. If only she hadn't been just sitting there watching Arlene dance and thinking she was almost as good as the kids on *Bandstand*.

"No, I don't feel like dancing."

"Oh, come on. Arlene's getting tired. She's stepping on my feet."

"Not right now. Maybe later."

"Come on. I promise not to bite."

"No, really."

"Okay, okay. Suit yourself." He turned slightly so that he was no longer facing her.

She huddled beside the stereo. She wished the record would end, then the next record and the next. She wished they could just sit and talk. But she had nothing to say to them, not just now. She was sorry she'd come over, as sorry as if they'd been making fun of her. At least if they had been, she'd know what to say to them. They wouldn't be asking her over again. She could be glad for that at least. She wished she could go downstairs and talk with Harriet, as she often did after school before

Dave got home. Harriet always had time for her.

It wasn't her fault she couldn't dance. As a little girl, she'd had bad feet and should have worn bulky corrective shoes. But she had enough trouble making friends as it was. That would ruin her. She cried all morning. "It's okay that Arlene wears those shoes. She has lots of friends. Why do I have to do everything Arlene does?" And they gave in and bought her loafers. Her mother should have known better.

She watched *Bandstand* mostly because the kids talked about their lives. In the fan magazines, she was especially drawn to the stories of girls like Connie Francis or Connie Stevens telling how shy they were, how few boys they'd dated, how insecure they'd been – before they became stars, that is. Even now they found it hard to believe all that was happening.

It was happening, though. They'd finally stopped dancing and were sprawled on the floor around a bowl of popcorn that Harriet had brought up and left. Then she went downstairs again. Some mothers knew enough to leave their kids alone, didn't try to butt in every moment to "organize the fun." She was so busy watching, wishing Harriet had stayed and imagining what it might have been like if she had, that it took a few minutes for her to get off the chair and join the others. They had to slide over to make room for her, and then she almost sat down between Marc and Carla, but Marc grabbed her arm and pulled her around to the other side of him.

"Salt and pepper don't mix," Dave was saying.

"What?" She slid farther back on the floor. Was this his way of telling her she didn't belong here or saying he was sorry they'd invited her over?

"Salt and pepper don't mix," he said again. "If you've got a band where black and white kids play together, nobody wants to listen to you. At least that's what the booking agents tell you."

"I didn't know you had a band."

"It's not really a band, I guess. We just sort of hang out and play together—Joe Jacobs, Marty Katz, Dan Lewis, Harvey Brown, and I. We could get really good, but no one will give us any work, so we don't really take it seriously."

"That's awful."

"One guy even told us that black kids have a different beat. Without even listening, he told us there was no way we'd ever sound good together."

Dave started imitating what the beat was, and the others joined in. She tapped her fingers on the floor a few times in a futile effort to keep up with them. Her hand formed a fist to contain itself.

"What makes them say that?" she asked, to get them talking again, to stop this singing that excluded her.

"I don't know," Dave said. "They just do, that's all. They all do."

"But it doesn't make any sense."

"You're telling *me* it doesn't."

"Why don't you play for them to prove it?"

"They wouldn't listen."

"Have you tried?" None of this was ever said in the fan magazines. There was a record of Bobby Rydell and Chubby Checker singing each other's songs. She'd assumed they were friends. Now she'd have to take Chubby out of her fantasies.

"They wouldn't listen," Dave said again.

"You have to push harder than that. You can't just give up that easily."

Arlene and Carla were shooting eye darts at her. Carla formed "Stop it" with her thin, meticulously lipsticked lips.

It was no use. She couldn't hang on Dave's every word and pretend she looked up to him because he was a boy. She simply didn't know how to play the game the way Carla and Arlene did.

𝄞 Arlene was exactly fourteen months older and lived exactly fourteen blocks away—short blocks, the ones that went north and south. Her mother loved Arlene—and not only because she was Auntie Sue's daughter. Her mother wished Arlene was her daughter. Didn't her mother always say, "Arlene does this, when will you do this? When will you do this, when will you do this, when will you do what Arlene does?"

Her mother would drag her over to Auntie Sue's, and Arlene would play nicely for a while. Then one of her friends would come over, and she and Arlene would do nothing but tease her. Dave did the same. They used to play kickball together in the church parking lot next door, but whenever one of his real friends came along, they'd stop. She learned to get the best of him, though. Just when he was having the most fun, when he was winning by a big margin, she'd get a stomach ache and have to go inside.

But since September she'd been in high school, and for the first time she was in classes with Arlene. There was no avoiding her. There was no escaping the sight of what Arlene really was, a phony little bitch like the other popular girls. Arlene was everything she didn't want to be. This was what her mother wanted. It was too much for her.

𝄞 She had to make this psychologist understand that she had plenty of friends. "Last Thursday I went to the sub shop with the gang after school. Then Carla called over the weekend, to check on a homework assignment, but it was really just an excuse to talk. Carla's a straight-A student. She'd never forget an assignment."

"How do you feel about all this?"

"It's a little hard for me still. I mean it's all so new to me. I'm not used to having friends, and I sometimes don't believe it's all happening. But it is. It really is. They're always asking me to join them, to go to the sub shop, to the movies. It feels really great. They're really accepting me. It's a little hard since I don't have a boyfriend yet, and they're all pretty much paired off, but they don't seem to mind including me. I've got a whole group, a whole circle of friends now. Really, I couldn't be happier."

There was an awkward silence, the same kind as at Dave's after she refused to dance, the kind that made her want to crawl into the woodwork.

"Look, I really don't understand what I'm doing here. I could be at the sub shop. They wanted me to come again today."

So there. I don't have to be here. I don't want to sit at this long table across from you, in your neatly pressed business suit. I could be talking to Harriet, and she never had to be paid for all the times she listened to me. She listened because she wanted to.

"I don't have any problems I have to work out. Not any more. I did, but that's over and done with. Things are going great now. I feel really, really accepted by people."

This psychologist shit was ridiculous. All he was doing was letting her talk on and on. He didn't even realize she was lying. And the room wasn't the kind you could pace in. She didn't feel comfortable there.

There was no break from the talking: lie after lie, friend after friend. Once she started, there was no getting out of it. At school she was surrounded by real people. Like it or not, they took over her fantasies. Fabe, Annette, Shelley, Frankie, even Bobby – they were too abstract, too far away now that she was in high school. But they would always be there.

What was she talking about? Every time the psychologist tried to get her talking about her parents, she said they were perfectly happy now that she had friends. They didn't like her going out so much, especially on school nights, but they were willing to give it a try for a while. They knew how much the friends meant to her. Aside from that, she didn't talk about her parents much.

The people would always be there. There was no escaping them, not so long as she was "healthy," not so long as she had to leave this office and walk to Grandma Dora's. Her father picked her up there on his way home from work. She had to walk past a sub shop—not the one Arlene, Carla, Marc, and the others went to. In reality, they never went to sub shops, didn't have a hangout, or at least not that she knew of, but a group of kids always hung out at this sub shop, and it was an easy model. It was also just a block away from Grandma Dora's. There was no avoiding it. And no avoiding her grandmother, either. "How did it go, honey? What did the doctor say, honey?" Questions she couldn't answer.

Walking slowly along the street, she tried to remember what she had just told the psychologist. Maybe there was some truth in it, after all. Maybe she did really like the kids who hung out at that sub shop. Maybe today she could walk past there and not go four blocks out of her way to circle around and avoid that corner. Maybe this once none of the kids would call out to her. Maybe if they laughed, she wouldn't hear them. Maybe riding home in her father's car, she wouldn't have to bury her head in her jacket as they drove by.

Still, she knew all about corners. They were where the wilder kids hung out after they'd spent all their money inside, the kids who didn't go home until late and didn't worry about getting yelled at, because their parents didn't care. She thought of the kids who used to hang out in front of the Ambassador Hotel on the Boardwalk when she was little—junkies her parents told her to stay away from, kids from South Philly. Those days formed an image in her mind of corners, all corners and all groups of kids, that she would never be able to break away from. She was terribly, uncontrollably afraid of them, so afraid that she cut around the corner a block earlier tonight to make sure they wouldn't spot her.

There was no use trying to explain this to her parents or to ask her father to pick her up at the psychologist's office. They'd only tell her to take the bus home, and she couldn't do that. There might be kids on the bus who'd stayed late at school – the worst kind, kids who'd been detained. There was no way her parents would understand. When no one called her and she had nothing to do all weekend, they kept bugging her to make some stupid sculptures. Again and again her parents told her how wrong she was: everyone liked her. She'd pledged for the sorority, been sick half the year and missed a lot of meetings, but she still got in eighteenth out of twenty-four. Her sorority sisters had said they were happy to initiate her and they wanted her to feel like one of them, and she was the only pledge who ever interrupted at that point to say thank you.

She was Annette's best friend, and she was Shelley's best friend. She was the link between them. She, Frankie, and Fabe were another trio, but she and Frankie were together first. How scared they had been when Fabe first joined them. He was only fifteen, they said, too young, still tied to his mother's apron strings. Frankie was nineteen. She imagined she was eighteen. Bob and Pete had their hands full just trying to set up engagements for the two of them. Now, with Fabe, their attention would be even more spread out. He wasn't a real threat to her. The clubs she sang in wanted a woman, not a man, but Fabe was definitely stepping onto Frankie's turf. Frankie felt threatened, and the two of them made it rough on Fabe. They would forget to introduce him to people. She and Frankie would get into a private conversation that excluded Fabe, the way Arlene and her friends often did to her. Fabe had to prove himself worthy of their friendship, and he did. But if it ever came right down to the wire, she knew it would be her and Frankie. They would stick by Fabe up to a point, but he hadn't been with them from the start. He hadn't been through all the hard times they had. Of course, Frankie had been managed by Bob and Pete before she came along. She was just as much a usurper, if Frankie wanted to see things that way, but he didn't.

𝄞 Of all the horrors of being in a sorority, the worst was having to go to the annual dance, having to ask someone. The blind date she had last year, with a friend of Richard's, was the only time she saw him. It was going to be better this year: she was a sophomore, a member and not a pledge, and she knew more people. And there was a boy she especially had her eye on. Ed, a senior, looked a little like Mike on *Bandstand*: thin, not tall but taller than she was. His curly black hair was long enough for a pompadour. He always wore dark blue or brown plaid shirts, tucked in, never hanging out. He was quiet enough to seem considerate and gentle, and he always paid attention to other people. He'd run for student-council president the year before and lost. She'd worked on his campaign. She'd stuck by him. He would be nice to her. Just a month before, he'd broken up with his girlfriend, so he was available.

Finally she had the nerve to call him. Her mother and father had finished dinner and were watching a TV quiz show in the kitchen while they loaded the dishwasher. She sat at the desk in the den and stared out the window. When they first moved here, they could see all the way to Ventnor Avenue from this window, before the neighborhood was built up. She held the receiver firmly against her ear and moved her neck and head around until she felt comfortable. She sat up tall in the hard wooden chair and dialed firmly.

No. Ed told her no. He said, "I'm afraid I can't. My grandmother died two weeks ago."

"So?"

"So it's still the mourning period. I wouldn't feel right about going to a dance."

"Oh. I'm sorry. I forgot."

"Otherwise I'd love to go with you. Maybe next time."

"Sure." She couldn't think of anything else to say to him.

"I'll see you in school next week," he said after a pause. That ended it.

She went with Jack, a boy she knew from summer school. He was only sixteen and already had what looked like a beer belly. His crew cut made him look as if he was in the army. He didn't belong to a fraternity. He'd told her that until he was in seventh grade, a lot of boys had called him a sissy, even though he'd been left back a year and was older than they were. She'd gone to the movies with Jack a few times, just because she had nothing better to do. But she'd turned him down a lot of times, too. He never gave up calling her. He'd be thrilled to take her to the dance.

Meet me at midnight,
Mary –
Same place
We always go.
Meet me at midnight,
Mary,
And don't let anyone know.

It was a song by some singer whose name she didn't know. When Jack picked her up before the dance, in his father's 1953 Plymouth, he turned on the radio, and that song happened to be playing. The need for secrecy appealed to him, the "don't let anyone know" – meaning his parents, her parents, the more popular kids at school he still had hopes of being friendly with. Its secrecy implied they were doing something forbidden, even though neither of them would have had the nerve, unless you counted kissing or going to a movie fifteen miles away to avoid people they knew, when the same picture was playing right in the neighborhood. Anyway, the song was important to him. "Let's make this our song," he said.

A month later Ed was going steady with Arlene. That was the final insult. She never again had the nerve to ask any boy to go out with her. She'd never again let boys laugh behind her back, as she imagined Ed must have been doing. Even so, she couldn't help thinking what might have happened if only Ed had said yes, if he'd gone steady with her instead of Arlene. All her anguish could have been avoided if only his grandmother hadn't died just then. From that point on, she wanted nothing more to do with family.

𝄞 On the Saturday after the dance, she got up late, dressed in jeans, mumbled a quick hello to her parents, and went next door to Harriet's. Harriet was kind. She didn't gossip like other women. It was easy to turn to Harriet, even though she was nearly her mother's age and her prematurely gray hair made her look even older.

Harriet sat at the kitchen table, drinking her third or fourth cup of coffee. As always, Harriet offered her some.

"Where's Dave?" she asked finally. Even though Harriet was Dave's mother, she knew she could trust her never to tell him anything.

"He went over to the ball field. What's wrong?" Harriet knew that whenever she was upset about something and needed to talk, she always asked first where Dave was, to make sure he wasn't about to walk in on them. "What's wrong?" she asked again, gently.

"I don't know, maybe nothing."

"That also means maybe something."

She bent her head and mumbled into her coffee, "I think I might have gotten pregnant after the dance last night. I'm not sure."

"What happened?"

"Well, we left the dance early, and we were just sort of sitting in Jack's car, and he took his penis out, and I was fondling it and all."

"Did you have your clothes off?"

"No, but my blouse was unbuttoned, and Jack was playing with my breasts."

"My God, sweetheart, don't you know anything about the facts of life? Didn't your mother ever talk to you?"

And when she just hung her head, Harriet explained everything she might someday need to know.

𝄞 As for that sorority key she'd worked so hard for, which she somehow thought would bring her instant popularity: the long pointed end was good for cleaning fingernails. Carla taught her that. Anyway, she was no longer picking her nose.

𝄞 She looked around her parents' living-room/dining-room combination as though for the first time: the round table with the chairs that couldn't go under because of their arms, the purple striped sofa against the wall and turning the corner, the one armchair to the right, and everything else pushed left. It was the perfect shape for pacing. The room used to have chairs jutting out in the middle, the wing sofa she'd get scolded for sliding down the arms of, the oblong dining-room table with its chartreuse leather chairs and grayish wood. That furniture took up all the space. It would have been impossible to pace in a room like that. It struck her as odd and unplanned but true: in 1960, the year her parents hired an interior decorator to furnish the living-room/dining-room combination, the fantasies began to take over her life. It was also the year her mother learned to drive, so she could get about on her own.

Now, in February 1964, her second year in high school, she wished her mother would stay away more and maybe get trapped in the business like her father. Working nine to five in the office was never enough now, not with her trapped at home all day long. Home was better than school, for the most part, but the choice was limited.

Pacing worked up the fever. At four o'clock every afternoon, before taking her temperature, she paced the living room for ten minutes, and she always had a fever. It never failed her. A half hour before, she had no fever. Pacing added an extra edge, safer than the sore throats she faked when she was nine, her way then of staying home and avoiding an arithmetic or geography test.

"Mononucleosis," the doctor called it. She refused to let him take blood from her arm, and she ended up in the hospital for ten days. "Overactive thyroid." The doctor knew she needed to get away from home and her mother. They kept finding new names for it.

CHAPTER FOUR

March – August 1964
Age fifteen

Songs in the Top Forty included
RAG DOLL
MY GUY
CHAPEL OF LOVE
EVERYBODY LOVES SOMEBODY

AT FIRST SHE WANTED TO GO to boarding school. She had her parents get all the catalogues, with their pictures of children her age having fun together. She was going to have fun too, she thought. As long as it was far from Atlantic City, she would be accepted anywhere. Look at all the new friends Richard had now that he was off at college, more friends than his sister, Arlene, even. She turned the pages of the catalogues and spent a long time concentrating on each picture. She liked the photos in black and white better. It was easier to fill in the details on her own. And somewhere in every catalogue was the one sentence she avoided thinking about: "Children with special needs receive special attention."

Yes, she had special needs. Even before she had her parents write for more information, she realized these were not real boarding schools but glorified mental hospitals. Her parents said as much themselves. They told her time and again that most boarding schools wouldn't accept her, not in midyear like this. She looked at the smiling children and realized they weren't really happy.

Then there was Dr. Freed's suggestion, the first time she and her mother went to Philadelphia to see him. No one in Atlantic City could help her now. Dr. Freed had silver hair, longer than she'd ever seen on a man, and a thin little silver beard to match.

"You ought to be someplace where you can finish school," he said. "There's a place in New York City where I've referred other patients your age, and they've had very good results with them: the New York State Psychiatric Institute." Only he pronounced it *sick*-iatric, as if to soften the word and at the same time tell her how sick she was, how sick he thought she was. It was only the first time he met her. And, of course, her mother did most of the talking.

"Do you really think it's necessary to put her in a hospital?"

"Not necessary, exactly. But she'd be able to finish school and get treatment at the same time."

There was a long pause. She stared out the window, at the snow out the window.

"I'm not sure they would accept her, of course," she heard him say. "But I'd like to start the application procedure. In the meantime, I can see her three times a week, and we'll see how that progresses."

"If that's what you think is best," her mother said. "We want to do the best for her. We just really don't know what to do."

"What do you want?" he asked her. It was the first time in ten minutes he'd acknowledged she was in the room. She was starting to forget herself, watching the snow through the barred window and thinking how scared her mother was of driving in weather like this. Even in the bus she was a nervous wreck and hadn't stopped talking the entire trip. It took twice as long in this weather, and the return trip would probably take even longer.

"What do you want to do?" he asked again.

"I don't care," she said. She felt tears welling up. Was she really that sick? She wanted to go home. She just wanted to go home. Hurrying through the vestibule into the waiting room, she had seen a woman with dyed red hair who looked really crazy sitting on the love seat. She didn't want to think about it.

They made an appointment for the following Monday. Four days away. She heard him saying goodbye to her. At last they were out of there.

She didn't want to go, didn't want to be around so many people, didn't want to be in a hospital. Sunday morning she was crying in her parents' bed, lying between them the way she had done as a little girl.

"I don't want to go there. Please, don't let them take me."

"The doctor thinks it's best."

"I don't care. I'm scared of hospitals. Please."

"You have to finish school."

"Not there. Please, not there. I'm really scared."

"We don't even know if they'll accept you yet."

"Please, don't send me there. Please."

"We'll talk to Dr. Freed about it. Maybe there's another way. Maybe he can keep on seeing you."

"Don't let them come and take me. Promise you won't let them come and take me."

And they promised they wouldn't.

𝄞 Troy Donahue used to spend summers in Ocean City. Only he had a different name then. At first it seemed good. Here was someone close to her. How far away was Ocean City? Ten or fifteen miles. But the more she thought about it, the harder it was to fit him into her world. She knew Ocean City too well. It was the one town in the area that was completely dry, even in restaurants. A lot of college kids worked there summers, having convinced their parents how safe they would be there. But then Somers Point, the next town, was nothing but bars, and they never asked for proof of age. Even high-school kids drank there. She had gone there once with a boy Richard had set her up with, and she had gotten sick to her stomach drinking apple brandy mixed with bitter lemon. It made her sick to think about it.

She hadn't changed her name once she'd become famous. She wanted to show all the people she'd grown up with that she'd made good. She was in Annette's swimming pool, having trouble swimming, as always. She gagged, her mouth filled with the awful taste of chlorine. Frankie stood there telling her to straighten her arms and kick her feet. "Come on, you can do it," he said. He was so gentle with her.

Troy Donahue didn't fit in this world. Oh, they were nice to him the one time they invited him over—they were nice to everyone—but they had nothing in common except their ages. He didn't sing. She thought of the one movie he'd starred in, *Parrish*, a long extravaganza about a boy trying to break with his family, a sort of *Gone with the Wind* made over teenage fashion. Even there she had nothing to relate to, though she watched it three times.

Her mother knew how much her daughter loved the stars. Or at least she suspected. She saw her hanging onto every word that Uncle Steve said. Well, she could give her daughter just as much. That's why she got the autograph: her daughter's name and then "All love from Patty Duke" and the date, May 6, 1964, on a cocktail napkin from Scottie's bar mitzvah. Scottie lived up the street. His father owned a motel half a block from the Steel Pier. Patty stayed there during her engagements the last three summers. She'd gotten friendly with Scottie then. Her mother pointed out that it was only natural that she should come down for his bar mitzvah, the luncheon her daughter wasn't invited to. Well, she never played with Scott, her mother pointed out. Anyway, here's the autograph. She shoved it in a drawer quickly, before she started to cry. Just one more reminder. How her mother thought Scott was such a lovely boy. How if she'd played with him, she too could have been invited. How things like knowing the stars only happened to other kids.

𝄞 It was probably the closest to a diner that Atlantic City had, on the order of the rowdy sub shops but more for adults than for kids: metal tables, a floor so stained you'd never get it clean, like the floor in her father's office, and a big old jukebox in the corner.

She hadn't been in that diner since she was in kindergarten and her aunt was dying. She and her mother were at her aunt's all the time, and this was the nearest place to grab something to eat. She remembered being afraid of the place. But Auntie Sue, Arlene's mother, liked it, even though her home and furniture were expensive and her cashmere sweaters came from the most exclusive shops. Auntie Sue had the sort of slow walk and manners that would have made a lot of women afraid, but Auntie Sue had stayed friendly with her old friend's husband and his second wife. She was still over there all the time and in the diner all the time. Today Richard was home from college. Auntie Sue and Arlene had dragged Richard and her mother along, and her mother had dragged her. She felt she'd be safe as long as Richard was there.

She ordered a hot dog and, as usual, gulped it down and was finished way before the others, a habit she'd picked up from Grandma Dora.

"I ran into Belle Katz in Needlecraft the other day," Auntie Sue said. "God, she's gotten old."

"She really ought to take better care of herself."

"I've heard that Mike's been seeing other women."

"I wouldn't be surprised."

"It's really a shame."

"I don't care how much she's let herself run down," her mother said. "There's still no excuse for his playing around."

"I'm not excusing it. I just say you can't really blame him."

"You know who else really looks old? Rhoda Nelson."

"God, I haven't seen her in years."

"She goes to the B'nai B'rith luncheons all the time."

"She really works hard there, doesn't she?"

"I think it's just an excuse to keep busy since Art died."

"It's still for a good cause."

"That's true," her mother said. "She's going to be nominated for secretary next year."

"Who's running against her?"

"Jeanne Lewis."

"I never liked Jeanne."

"She seems to think she's better than the rest of the world."

"I knew her and Milton when they had no money," Auntie Sue said. "Milton was working two jobs just to make ends meet."

"It's amazing how quickly people forget where they came from. Lynn Cohen's the same way."

"Lynn was that way even before she had money."

"People don't really change, I guess."

"At least Lynn dresses well."

"She buys all her clothes in New York. I hear she knows the best designer outlet shops."

"I heard an outlet shop might be opening in Pleasantville."

"I don't have the stamina to shop in outlet shops," her mother said. "I need time to try things on and see how I feel in them. I hate to be rushed."

"I don't mind. I'd rather buy things quickly. I don't have time to potske."

"Homberger's should be having their spring sale pretty soon."

"Edith always loves to shop there."

"The trouble with stores like that is they don't have a large stock. You meet yourself coming and going."

"I've found Ronette's is a fairly good shop. I bought the blue cotton shirtwaist I wore to the Lions' dinner last week there."

"That really looked good on you," her mother said. "You have a thick neck, and it's really best when you can wear open collars."

"Lynn has an even thicker neck than I do."

"She's also taller, though."

Her head was splitting. She went to the bathroom and on the way back glanced at the jukebox. They had all the tunes from the artists you'd expect – Connie Francis, Frank Sinatra, Pat Boone, Paul, Frankie, Bobby. They were old songs, none of the newer releases, which were probably too expensive for a place like this.

That was when she spotted the record by Marty, Uncle Steve's protégé: "Tomorrow, My Friend" and "In Love with Love." On a jukebox! In Atlantic City! She wanted to jump up and down with joy. She wanted to call out to her mother and her mother's high-class friend or to Arlene and Richard at least. That would show them. That would teach them not to whisper about Uncle Steve's useless dreams. She should have played the record for them. It would have been so easy to push D-6, D-8. Except she didn't have the nerve. Harriet was the only person she told about seeing Marty's record there, and that was two days later.

𝄞 "Here I am, Bobby, here. In Atlantic City. Steel Pier, third row center for all your shows. Standing in line for your autograph. Sleeping just three miles away from you. Bobby, look here."

It was really true, wasn't it? Bobby really *was* searching all over the big, big world for a "little bitty girl." For the first time in her life, she was glad she had never hit the five-foot mark.

Only he wasn't looking. She couldn't blame him, really. Who would think to look in Atlantic City? There was nobody here, no "swinging school." Still, he'd chosen to première the song at the Steel Pier. It was more than chance. She knew it was. He must have spotted her.

But, of course, he'd recorded that song because of her, to begin with. Like Annette's "Tall Paul," when she was dating Paul, really a head shorter. It was Bobby's secret message to her, his way of telling the whole world how much he loved her.

"Here I am, Bobby, here. I'm dancing with you." Even though with the cha-cha you barely touch, we don't care about style, alone here in my apartment. We slow the pace down slightly. I put my arms around your waist and lean my head on your chest, and your arms enclose all of me, like a black couple I saw on *Bandstand* once. You sing the words softly, just for me: "I've got such a big, big love for this little bitty girl." Yeah, yeah.

𝄞 "Well, what was I supposed to say?" Bobby laughed. "That I really don't want to meet any more dream girls because I've already found you? A lot of new fans *that* would get me." He put his arm around her.

"But what was that about not liking ponytails?" She playfully banged on the coffee table. It was written right there in his most recent interview: "I really can't stand that pinched look they give your face." Bobby knew very well that she always wore her hair in a ponytail around the house.

"Well, I had to throw them a curve," he laughed. "We agreed we wouldn't let the gossip columns have a field day with us, didn't we?"

She laughed too, but then she checked herself. After all, the next sentence read, "Another thing that irks me is a girl who laughs too loud." True or not, she wasn't taking any chances.

Bobby's arm was still around her. She leaned back and laid her head on his shoulder. Fan magazines! They were always making something out of nothing, but let's face it: either you let them play with your life or you stood no chance of becoming a star. They understood that she, Bobby, Frankie, Fabe, Paul, Annette, Shelley. They all understood that was the difference between them and the older entertainers. They were willing to reach out to their fans, kids their own age, who really needed them. Their managers worked hard to build up the image of good, clean-cut kids. Being caught with a cigarette once could wreck their careers, and they knew it.

They went on dates with fans as publicity stunts and were photographed licking ice-cream cones or holding hands. Last summer in Florida, Fabe sat on the beach with a girl he'd met, and Bob Marcucci snuck up on them just as he was kissing her. Poor Fabe still hadn't heard the end of that one. "What if I'd been a photographer or a reporter after a story?" Bob was still screaming a week later. "Some of those magazines dig up dirt enough. We don't have to feed them any material." Of course, the fact that Bob himself had snuck off with this girl's friend didn't matter. Fabe was the star, not him. Up to a certain point, Bob didn't have to worry about his image.

That's what was good about sitting in her apartment with Bobby. They didn't have to worry about people sneaking up on them. And even Bob and Pete were considerate enough to call before they came over. They had keys to her apartment, but they still called, even if only from the telephone downstairs. Frankie Day, Bobby's manager, wasn't that thoughtful. She'd never been overly fond of Frankie to begin with, and after that night when he'd found them together at Bobby's, she simply tried to avoid him. Bobby tried to smooth things over, of course. He felt the same way about Frankie Day as she felt about Bob and Pete. For his sake she bit her tongue and smiled when she saw him. Bobby had said right in the article that he wanted a "happy" girl, and she knew that dwelling on the matter would make things tense between them. That's what everyone adored about Annette and Shelley. They could have fun even in the most difficult circumstances. She would make herself be that way, too.

𝄞 No matter what she had or what she did, it was always wrong. A boy in her seventh-grade class became the most popular kid at school after he brought his electric guitar to a class party. As for her, when she played "Camptown Races" on her accordion in *The Pied Piper* at summer camp, all the kids in the bunk called her a showoff.

All summer she'd practiced a full hour every day, instead of her usual forty-five minutes. She'd worked hard to memorize the song, following the metronome her teacher always set going. That whole summer, not once did he rap her fingers for losing the beat. At the performance, she even stood up straight and balanced herself, so she didn't tip backward when she moved the bellows too quickly.

She'd been studying for three years, ever since fourth grade. She'd learned all the simple tunes and marches and polkas: "The Marine's Hymn," "*La Donna è Mobile*," "Drink to Me Only with Thine Eyes," "The Caissons Go Rolling Along." In a few months, the teacher promised, she'd be playing well enough to try songs like "Carnival of Venice," "Sharpshooters," and "Storm Echoes Overture."

Frankie and Bobby worked their instruments into TV appearances and club dates, and the audiences ate it up. Frankie even did a trumpet solo on his second album. It showed how versatile he was. She pictured herself lugging that fifty-pound accordion around with her like a suitcase, sitting on it in bus stations as if she had no better place to be, strapping it across her small breasts, and bending over to pick it up or put it down. Some teen angel she'd make! That was why she never mentioned her accordion lessons. She never thought about those few weeks when she got everything right, and the teacher, for a special treat, wrote out songs like "Puppy Love" and "Venus," which she could practice only in her spare time.

But sometimes, to illustrate something to Bob or Pete, she'd play a few notes on the piano with her right hand on the keys that were the same as on the accordion. They never questioned that – nearly all middle-class kids studied piano at one time or another. They never asked to hear more. When she was at one of the rare jam sessions, when Bobby was playing drums and Frankie trumpet along with some of the guys who used to play with them in the old days, she had the sense to keep her mouth shut about playing accordion. Even if she could have sight-read music, even if she could have kept a perfect beat, she wouldn't have fit in. Accordions were Lawrence Welk music. They would have laughed at her, the way they joked about the Lennon sisters. As much as she loved them all, as comfortable as she felt with them, she couldn't risk that.

𝄞 "What time's your doctor's appointment?" Uncle Steve asked.

"One-thirty."

"So you're finished when? Two-thirty?"

"Two-fifteen." They were in the car driving from Atlantic City to Philly.

"Good. I'm hoping my meeting won't take too long. Sometimes they throw a two-hour sales pitch at us."

How well she knew that. She had memory after memory of shivering in the doorway of Wannamaker's waiting for him to pick her up, when he was an hour or more late. On other days, she was five minutes late, and he was at the curb already, complaining that the meeting was over early and he could have left an hour ago.

"Better call me as soon as you're out of the doctor's," he said. "I want to leave as early as possible today."

"Sure. What's up?"

"Oh, I thought I told you last week. Frankie Avalon's appearing at the Latin Casino. I want to stop off at the motel down the road where he always stays. I have some papers to drop off for him. Maybe spend some time talking. I haven't seen him for over a year now."

"Didn't you see him in Atlantic City last summer?"

"No, it was right before the Fourth of July. I had too many customers breathing down my neck. It's always a big time for liquor sales."

"What a mess."

"You're telling me. Another year or two and maybe I'll be out of debt enough to quit this job."

"Great." How many years had she been listening to her parents argue about Uncle Steve fooling around when he was supposed to be working?

"I just hope that meeting won't take too long," he said again.

She held her breath and prayed he wouldn't get tied up. For half a moment she considered telling him she could take the bus home, to beg out before he let her know she wasn't wanted. But she was too scared he'd agree.

She told Dr. Freed, "We've made plans. Provided my uncle doesn't get tied up at the meeting, we'll have dinner with Frankie and then maybe take in the show."

And he didn't get tied up. He picked her up in Center City at quarter past four on the dot and pushed through the rush-hour traffic with fewer curses than usual. An hour later they pulled into the motel parking lot. "Wait here," he said. He grabbed some papers off the dashboard, got two bottles of Scotch from the back seat, and was off.

He was back five minutes later, empty-handed. "He was in, but he's sleeping. I didn't want to disturb him, so I left everything for him at the desk."

They started home in silence. She thought about what it would have been like to meet Frankie and what she would tell the doctor. Probably Uncle Steve was thinking something of the sort, because his mind seemed to be wandering, and he forgot to keep checking in the rearview mirror for cops. Sure enough, there was a siren. They pulled over. Uncle Steve got out of the car and talked to the cops. Then he came back and took out two more bottles of Scotch, just like the ones he'd left for Frankie.

𝄞 Open, vulnerable, and invariably stomped on, she sang of young love. She sang her heart out, like the other women rockers, pleading songs like "Please Love Me Forever" or "I Want to Be Wanted," or, as in Shelley's hit tune, she sat and dreamed of "Johnny Angel," who didn't even know she existed. She knew it was the girls who bought records, and a woman's only hope of making the Top Forty was to express the hopes of the teenyboppers and be weak, docile, and oh so terribly innocent.

How well the role suited her. She was all of seventeen. Technically she'd run away from home, even if her parents did know where she was, and she didn't have to worry they'd come looking for her. She was a young seventeen, at that. She needed to be taken care of. Once in a while she wondered what would happen if, during an argument with Bob, she stood up and argued her point, instead of whining and playing the hurt little girl. But she was afraid to try, as if she were afraid of winning, afraid of finding out how strong she really was.

There had been another test today. There was a meeting to discuss an engagement at the Latin Casino. She'd always wanted to sing there, close to both Philly and Atlantic City. Her parents had gone to fund-raising shows there for the Lions and B'nai B'rith. Her appearance there would be the final proof that she'd made it.

The representative shook hands with Bob, then with her. "It's all set," he said. "We'll send you the contracts in a week or two."

Bob was a little thrown when the rep didn't pull the contracts out of his desk drawer right then, like most reps, but he was submissive. She needed more than that. Without thinking, she went into her little-girl act. "Can't we sign the contracts now?" Her voice automatically rose an octave.

"I don't have them made up yet," he said in a preoccupied monotone.

"Can we wait?" Tears were filling her eyes. "This engagement's really important to me. My family lives near there."

"I give you my word it'll go through. Why isn't that enough for you?"

"I've had dates canceled on me before. Please, this is really important to me."

"I shook on it, didn't I?"

She didn't respond, just stood there wide-eyed and innocent.

"Look, if we draw up the contract now, I'll have to give you a check today," the rep said. "I'm not authorized to do that yet."

"No, you won't. I'll even sign a separate agreement that I don't need the advance till two weeks before the date."

He thought for a moment. She was backing him into a corner, and they both knew it. Let there be no doubt, though: he wanted control here. Things had to be done on his terms, not hers. He liked throwing his weight around. You could see in his eyes how much he liked it. "I'll tell you what. Let me talk to my boss and confirm the date," he said. He handed her a second business card, as if that was a contract. "Give me a call tomorrow morning, and if the date's clear, I'll draw up the contract then."

She acted relieved as she shook his hand again. Bob all but pushed her out of the office. In the safety of the hall, they both sighed in relief. The deal wasn't confirmed yet, but she felt better than she had half an hour ago.

Bob's reassuring arm pressed against her shoulder. The thought crossed her mind to pull away, stare him straight in the face, and give him one hell of a tongue-lashing for not standing up for her. It was the manager's job to secure the contract, not hers. What the hell was she paying him fifteen percent for?

But her body drew closer to him, and her arm folded itself

across the back of his waist, almost shoulder height for her. She laughed when she caught a glimpse of them reflected in the metal trim along the corridor. Their embrace suggested the sexual, teenybopper style – a kiss on the cheek but a kiss nonetheless. Older women slept with their managers, and the women who played the nightclub circuit slept with any number of booking agents. No, it was better this way. She wanted to be a little girl forever.

𝄞 She wanted to grow up and perform in Vegas and all the first-rate nightclubs, to get past the dinner-theater stage, as Frankie and Bobby had.

It wasn't what Bobby sang that was important. It was what he said: we'd gone from the stone age to the rock age, and each generation refuses to appreciate the songs of previous and later generations. But really the songs of the forties weren't all that bad. He could appreciate songs like "Mammy" and "Cement Mixer Putty-Putty." Singing a few of those songs, he proved himself to this older audience, and only after that did he ask them to listen to his own hit songs. The applause was enormous.

This wasn't *Bandstand* or the Steel Pier. These weren't girls in bobbysocks tearing his sweater. He had a tuxedo on. This was the Copa, New York City's most famous nightclub. Bobby Rydell had waited all his life to appear here, and now that he'd turned eighteen, it was finally possible. She knew how much it meant to him: if he was accepted by this crowd, it would ensure his future as an entertainer. He even did impersonations. Someone in the back of the room whistled at his Clem Kadiddlehopper. He impersonated Bobby Darin, the only young rock singer who'd already established himself with this adult audience. They loved it. He said Bobby Darin was a real good friend of his. She knew better, of course, but he did it for the applause, and he got away with it.

She listened to his album, imagined herself sitting at a table to the right of the stage, with his parents, Frankie Day, Dick, and a few others, his closest friends. His first-night jitters were making her stomach rumble, and one glass of Coke was going to her head as if it were wine. The applause after his first medley, though, put both of them at ease.

Beside her, Bobby's mother had tears in her eyes. She reached under the table and clasped Mrs. Ridarelli's hand for a moment, squeezed it reassuringly. This night meant even more to Mrs. Ridarelli than it did to Bobby. Her son was making it in the eyes of her generation, kidding around about his youth, saying his babysitter crooned him to sleep with this song and that song "takes me way back to my high-school freshman days." People the age of her parents gave him a standing ovation. And in another nine months she too would be old enough to appear in the Copa. If she could just sing as well as this, maybe her parents would believe in her. She prayed to God they wouldn't hold Bobby up as an example of someone who'd done it better, the way they'd done with Arlene all the time. Don't take Bobby's friendship away from her.

𝄞

Every time she was sick, her old fears came back. People accepted her only because she was always in there plugging. If she missed one date, she would no longer be wanted. "I've got to do the show," she told Bob. Unintentionally, the scratch in her throat made it sound like a growl.

Bob burst out laughing. "You've got to be kidding."

"Please."

"The way you sound, they'd only laugh at you."

"I'll be lip-synching. Remember?"

"You look awful."

"I'll fix myself up. Just wait and see."

"It's *Bandstand*, for Christ's sake. You've done it a hundred times already, and you'll do it a hundred times more. Why's this once so important?"

She didn't answer. The tears in her eyes were only partly from her cold. What with the fever too, she looked like a waif, and Bob couldn't help laughing again – with her, not at her.

"I know, baby," he said finally, putting his arm around her. "But the most important thing right now is to get you well. Dick would want that too."

Gradually she let herself be convinced. It was hard, though: all her life, sickness had been an escape. She'd faked stomach aches and sore throats to get out of things and to convince herself she wasn't needed. Even now it was hard to believe people cared. Then all the old symptoms came back, and it was impossible to believe she wasn't still faking it. And she wasn't the only one who felt that way.

"What's the use?" Fabe folded his arms on the table and leaned his chin on them, unconsciously falling into one of those poses that photographers were always trying to push him into. With only two or three hours of sleep, fighting to keep his eyes open, Fabe was even more of a lady-killer than usual.

"Don't forget Bobby had to take acting lessons, too," she said.

"*After* he got the part."

She sat silent, patient. Whatever she might have said wouldn't have helped much. She reached across the small round table and rested her hand inside his folded arms.

She'd been half-expecting something like this. The night before, they'd all gone to the première of *Bye Bye Birdie* – she,

Frankie, Fabe, Bob, Pete, Dick, Annette, Shelley, Paul, Frankie Day, and Bobby – a group of old friends, like any other group, to see Bobby's first movie. Then they'd stayed up half the night celebrating.

She knew how badly Fabe had wanted that part. Last night his smile had been forced, his laughter a little louder than usual. She understood why it was hard for him. That's why she'd decided to sleep on his couch, saying she was too tired to drive home.

"They said I couldn't sing," Fabe said. "Two singing teachers rejected me before Pete taught me himself, so I worked hard at the lessons, and the girls went crazy when I walked on stage. Then I studied acting and got movie parts, bit parts with star billing, just to be sure the kids would come. I danced a circle around Bing Crosby, with only ten lines in the whole script. Beach flicks, a TV show here and there, a couple of 'down-home' movies when I've lived in Philly all my life. Some girl even wrote to *Teen* advising me to quit. They won't give me a chance to act."

And here was Bobby, in his first movie, not only in the starring role but on camera most of the time and with enough songs to fill an album. She'd been happy for him. Bobby had worked hard for this. He'd been crushed when he wasn't chosen for the Broadway play. Once he got settled working again, she knew, Fabe would be happy for Bobby, too. They'd all but grown up together.

Fabe had to talk to her because she wasn't from the old neighborhood. Frankie, Bobby, Dick, Bob, Pete – they all knew him too well. Their families knew each other, and half of them went to church together. As preteens, Bobby and Frankie had been in the same band, Rocco and the Saints. She thought of all the times the guys got reminiscing about it and she'd felt excluded. Fabe couldn't talk to Paul easily, and he'd never been close to Annette or Shelley. She was the only one he could turn to now. She hadn't been there, and he didn't have to be ashamed with her.

Even so, her loyalties were divided. She loved Bobby more than she ever let on. He was the better entertainer, and that role had been right for him. But Fabe was reaching out to her. She had to be there, if only to pour some coffee into him. By tomorrow they'd both be back at work as hard as ever – lessons, interviews, rehearsals, photo sessions. Bobby would be down from his star trip and back in the old routine again. This morning would be forgotten, pushed aside by a thousand more important things, but it would stay in the back of their minds somewhere.

She walked around the table behind Fabe and draped her arms over him. He opened up then and drew her down on his lap. They sat without speaking, his head buried in her breast like a little boy's, her head on his shoulder. "I'm a man," he had sung over and over on his first record. No, he wasn't. Neither of them was as mature as they were forced to act sometimes. That was the hard part. That was what the fan magazines could never quite capture, try as they might to make them seem like normal teenagers. They were still childish and jealous and envious and anxious. It was this immaturity that, in the end, drew them closer to each other.

𝄞 Even Harriet said it wasn't good for her to stay alone, cooped up in the house all day, typing addresses on envelopes for a penny apiece for one of her father's friends so she'd feel useful. She should have contact with people her own age or maybe a little younger. Everyone thought that if they found kids weaker than she was, kids she could feel she was helping, then maybe she wouldn't feel threatened by them. The psychologist hit on the perfect solution: the Children's Seashore Home, a hospital and school for kids crippled by polio or arthritis, brain-damaged kids, kids with a hundred different physical problems. Every Tuesday night Brian Ginetti, a guy in his forties who taught at her old grammar school, went there to play ball games that encouraged the kids to use their limited reflexes. He always needed help. Would she, please?

Well, her mother would help. It was just like those days when her mother would drag kids home for her to play with, thinking maybe if she involved herself, her daughter would do the same. It worked, too. They even got Arlene to go along sometimes.

Mainly she related to the older kids, eleven and twelve years old. There was Larry, a sixteen-year-old who was brain-damaged. When he was little, he used to repeat whatever he heard adults say, and until he was five, everyone thought he was a genius. Larry had been in her first-grade class, and she remembered he used to wet his pants. Then there was Peggy, a twelve-year-old with a thin, misshapen body. She usually found Peggy in bed with weights on her arms and legs. Peggy's parents never visited. Peggy adored her, and many nights the two of them spent the whole time playing catch. One night when Peggy was depressed, she tickled her.

She liked Anna best. Anna was eleven years old and wore a pendant with a Catholic saint on one side and ROMA engraved on the back. Usually she was up and walking around, and she didn't look terribly sick, but she must have been in pain. Anna had a quiet sadness that she'd never seen in anyone before. Sometimes Anna let out an almost unconscious grunt when she caught a ball, as if it hurt to clasp her fingers. One night Anna didn't feel up to leaving the ward, so they just perched on her bed and talked.

"Do you really live right in the middle of South Philly?" she asked Anna.

"Yeah."

"Right where all the singers come from?"

"You bet. My family goes to the same church as Fabian's, Frankie Avalon's, and Bobby Rydell's. Ridarelli – that's his real name. I sort of know them. I mean I talked to them a few times, before they got famous." Anna had perked up for the first time that evening.

"Do you have their records?"

"Oh, sure. Only they're all back at home. I really miss them. I used to lie in bed and listen all the time. I wish I'd thought to bring them here."

So the next week, for a surprise, she showed up with three albums, by Bobby, Frankie, and someone she couldn't remember later. Just a loan. She didn't even think to check first whether Anna would be able to play them in the hospital. She placed them on Anna's shelves. It was hard to remember exactly what happened after that: she must have gone back a few times, because she remembered talking to Anna about Frankie's album. Then she started feeling insecure and self-conscious again, as if people could see through her, right into her fantasies. So she stopped going. She must have left the albums there.

CHAPTER FIVE

September 1964 – November 1966
Ages fifteen to seventeen

Songs in the Top Forty included
DOWNTOWN
THIS DIAMOND RING
STOP! IN THE NAME OF LOVE
HANG ON SLOOPY
EVE OF DESTRUCTION

She refused to listen to the Beatles.

AT ONE POINT THERE WAS talk of her doing a duet with Fabe, only she decided against that. She knew that when you have two, there was always the chance of ending up with three, and whenever you have three, there was always one left out, and she was always the one. Someone like Dick, who really cared about people, would be sure to get every member introduced, but even he often forgot their names by the time of their next appearance. No, she would go it alone, make it or break it for herself alone and not feel guilty. She wanted to be sure she would be remembered. Instead, some anonymous girl sang on Fabe's record as a sort of chorus: "Oooo-ooooo-ooooo-ooooh, Fabian."

Groups were something like baseball teams. She'd learned to enjoy baseball because it was something to talk about with her father. They'd make a day of it, driving up to Phillies games on Sundays and stopping to eat at the Chuckwagon in Cherry Hill on the way home. Or she'd make a late doctor appointment on a Friday, so she could go up with her father instead of her uncle, and they'd take in the game that night, even though he had to get up for work at six o'clock the next morning. Aside from baseball, they had nothing in common.

"Who's pitching tonight?" she asked one Friday. She already knew, but there was nothing else to say, and those long silences in the car were almost unbearable. She knew he was thinking about how sick she was. That's what he was always thinking about.

"Jim Bunning."

"Great."

Silence again.

"I'll still never forgive you for not wanting to drive up to Shea that day Bunning ended up pitching his perfect game," she said.

"New York's too far to drive for just a game."

"Two games. It was a doubleheader."

"We'd have gotten home too late."

"Anyway, Bunning's my favorite pitcher. Though Short's good too. Or at least he used to be."

"Short always has trouble with his arm late in the season. A lot of southpaws do."

"Yeah, but they're going to need him to clinch the pennant."

"The Phillies have been pretty lucky with injuries this year, when you stop to think of it. Bobby Wine got hurt, but if he hadn't, they'd probably never have discovered how good Rojas is."

"Rojas is incredible," she said. "Wherever they put him, he

does a great job. I wish they'd let him play third base now that Wine's back."

"Ritchie Allen plays there."

"Allen makes too many errors."

"They need his hitting."

"I don't like Allen. God, he even swung a bat at Callison once during warm-up."

"You have to think about what the team needs, not about individual players," her father said.

"I still don't like Allen."

"That doesn't mean he shouldn't be playing. Look at all the home runs he's hit. And he'll probably be nominated for Rookie of the Year. You can't damn a man just because you don't happen to like him."

"What about Rojas? Is it fair not to play him now, after he came through when they really needed him?"

"That's the way teams work."

"I still think it's ridiculous. Poor Rojas." She didn't care how many home runs Allen hit. She didn't care what her father said. She'd singled out Allen to pick on, and she was determined to pick on him. There had to be one in every group.

That silence again. Her father was probably thinking about how sick she was, wondering if she'd ever get well, if she'd ever learn that you had to make certain sacrifices in order to get along with other people. Teamwork, he called it.

So here they were again, right back where they started. She would go through the summer talking to her father, going to games with her father. It was better than nothing. In November he tried to interest her in football, but that never worked. It was too hard to identify with the players.

Look at Dion, singing with the Belmonts. Then he went out on his own and had hit after hit. He had a lot of courage. She bought his records, called him Di. He often came over to Annette's on the weekends. If he'd been on his own from the start, he would have been one of their gang, but he had others then, and by the time he was on his own, they had gotten, despite themselves, a little cliquish. She liked him, though. She sang his songs sometimes:

When I was sixteen,
Ran away,
All alone
On the stray.
What can I do?
What can I say?
I'm a lonely teenager.

I want to go home
Where I belong
'Cause now I'm just a
Lonely teenager.

Running away was something she was thinking about more and more. It just might be an alternative to suicide.

Tears filled her eyes when she read Paul Anka's confession of running away from home at fourteen. His family knew he wanted to be a singer, but they didn't understand, not really. He got as far as the bus station, sprawled out on a bench, and thought he'd sleep until the bus came. His father came first, of course, to tell him he understood now. He had understood all along and had been saving money to finance his career, he said. Just wait and finish school first, he said. He said his mother was at home crying. He said Paul was going to be punished, but Paul never told if he was or how he was.

She didn't have great dreams. She only had fantasies. How could she tell her parents of her imagined talent as a singer? They'd just point to some object she'd made when she was a kid, cans or boxes glued together, and tell her for the thousandth time what a talented sculptor she was. "You don't have to *imagine* talent," they would tell her. "You just don't want to take advantage of the talent you really have." Paul's parents had paid to get him started in his career. Her parents' money was wasted on her doctor bills.

She liked Paul better after she read his story. He was the sort of person who hardly ever admitted he was wrong, but now she knew all his cockiness was a cover. She knew how hard it must have been for him. But she couldn't tell him about herself. Bob and Pete had been very careful to cover up the story of her running away from home. Only Frankie, Fabe, and Annette knew, and they were like family anyway.

She saw herself sitting on the cold bench at the bus station. She didn't dare lie down. She covered her face when she saw anyone come in. She waited. Surely her father would come to get her soon. Either that or she'd run into that bus driver she'd once promised to meet in a hotel. She'd go along with whoever came first, she told herself.

She would run away from home, but she was afraid that the ticket clerk would know her and call her parents. This town was so small everyone knew everything about everybody. It was useless trying to reason with her parents. They would never understand the way Paul's parents did. Oh, they wanted her to "better herself," like all parents in Atlantic City, but the only way they understood of doing that was by going to college and then marrying a rich husband, a doctor or a lawyer. She'd already missed two years of school, and they'd given up hope of her ever doing that. Even if she *was* a sculptor or something, that probably wouldn't be good enough for them. They simply made the best of the things they couldn't change, the way they kept telling her to do. This house she hated, yet hid in, was all they ever wanted out of life. She was living in one room of her parents' house, keeping the curtains drawn and the door locked, eating her meals alone. And yet she was supposed to build a house for her parents now that she was famous.

"Come and see my new home," the cover story said. And inside, a smiling Frankie was holding the door open for his mother. Or, in another magazine, a beaming Mrs. Avallone took you through the house her son built for her. Four separate picture stories appeared on that house. Boy grows up poor, makes a million, and the first thing he does is build a house for his poor, devoted parents. The magazines loved it. It was the perfect image.

They laughed about Frankie building his parents their dream house, but it was out in the suburbs – the magazines were careful not to say it was in Cherry Hill – and too far away for him to commute. He stayed in their old South Philly row house when he was in town. The whole concept of them sharing the house together, one big happy family now, was a hoax to begin with. Frankie didn't get along with his parents all that much better than she did with hers, even though they kept in touch. They'd supposedly "encouraged" his career, dragging him from performance to performance as a child, their sole support after his father lost his job. Really, he built that house to be rid of them, though he didn't admit that even to himself.

Still, you could see his parents loved that house. They bought expensive paintings, Cézannes and Gauguins. They bought white shag carpet for the living room and the kinds of decorations Uncle Steve would have bought if he'd had the money. Her parents? Even in an expensive house, they'd probably fill it with Formica furniture and schlock prints of seascapes, the kind you saw at the boardwalk art shows.

No, she wasn't going to build a house for her parents, no matter how hard Bob coaxed. She could feel it coming, with all the play he was getting off Frankie, with Fabe talking of a house and now with Dick in the process of building one. She didn't want to give her parents anything and didn't expect a thing in return. Her growing up had been different. If she'd been Italian, there would have been a sense of family. But in Atlantic

City the Italian families were poor, in the minority, and looked down on. It had been a difficult adjustment for her when she'd first gotten friendly with people like Bob and Frankie, but she was happy now. She was accepted, and she wasn't going back. No need to drag her parents up here with her. They were content in the lives they chose and expected her to choose.

As for where she lived, she knew it had large windows facing the street, and she never drew the curtains. There was a baby grand piano in the living room, instead of the accordion tucked away in a closet. Aside from that, she didn't think about what the house was like. She wasn't there all that much. She was always over at Annette's or Fabe's, letting their mothers cook for her.

𝄞 She was crying, crying uncontrollably, a soft, quiet crying. She wasn't more than twenty pages into *I Never Promised You a Rose Garden*, and here she was crying over people she didn't know, crying in a way she never was able to cry about her own life. It was ridiculous. She had to stop this. Her parents would be home soon. She had to pull herself together.

She didn't cry through the whole book, though – only at the beginning and the end and a short part in the middle about how Deborah's mother and father were taking this and about the effect it had on her sister, who was three years younger. No, five years younger. It was her own sister who would have been three years younger, if her mother hadn't miscarried because they lived on the fourth floor and she always made her mother carry her up the stairs. If she'd had a real sister, she wouldn't have needed to live in her own world so much.

Deborah Blau told Dr. Fried she had tried to kill her sister.

She laughed at the similarities: their doctors had the same name only spelled differently, Deborah's mother had the same name as her mother, and she had really succeeded in killing her sister. It was nothing more than coincidence. Dr. Freed had wanted her to read it, though. She had read the other book he recommended, *David and Lisa*, and nothing had happened. But *I Never Promised You a Rose Garden* intruded upon her. Deborah was really sick and yet too close for comfort. She read about the Kingdom of Yr, Deborah's secret world, which had brought her at last to the hospital. It seemed childish when it was written out. It was easy to see why Deborah needed it, but it didn't help much. She knew now why she kept Frankie, Fabe, Dick, and the others hidden, even from her doctor. Oh, he knew that there was a place she went to when she paced and that she had friends there, but she never dared to let him in on its secrets. The book only confirmed her choices. Surely he hadn't intended that.

Deborah had said at first that she would see her mother but not her father. Not *him*. She didn't use his name. If they ever sent her away, she thought, that's how she would do it. She read about his hurt and cried because it seemed to describe her father's hurt. Men didn't understand, and yet the last thing she wanted was to be a woman. To be, God forbid, like her mother. To buy friends for her daughter the way Deborah's mother did. To become leader of the Brownies and invite kids over for lunch on Saturdays, only to have a daughter who refused to eat and had a second-grade teacher who dumped the messy contents of her desk on the floor and made her stay after school to clean it instead of going to the Brownie meeting. To instigate a bubble-blowing contest when her daughter couldn't blow bubbles. To buy friends for her daughter and have no friends of her own.

When she was three or four years old, a woman on the street sometimes said she looked like her mother, and she stomped her feet and screamed that she looked like her father. A little kid could get away with that sort of thing, but now she was sixteen, and everyone wanted her to go to the doctor and get well or normal and grow up to have children of her own. She could never do to a child what had been done to her. She would never be responsible. She could raise a child already born perhaps, but she never wanted that guilt of life on her conscience. Her period had stopped two years ago. If it ever started again, she would have her tubes tied. It would be safer that way. The world might be less of a threat to her.

Deborah was moved up to the disturbed ward and was happier there. It meant she could leave her hair uncombed and scream if she wanted, give up the pretense of normality that was needed in the other wards. Deborah had acted normal while she lived at home. Not her: she lived in her parents' house and acted like Deborah in the hospital, pretending she was even more disturbed than Deborah was, right in front of the neighbors, to punish her parents, maybe, for not sending her away. No, for giving birth to her.

She turned to Bob and Pete for comfort. Bob kept saying that sooner or later she'd have to face her parents again. Only she wasn't ready yet. She knew the burden she was placing on him, and yet she couldn't stop herself. It never dawned on her, though, that he would go behind her back, get in contact with them – not until they suddenly showed up in town. She almost blacked out in Bob's office. The familiar walls were suddenly bare of her two gold records and Frankie's five, bare of certificates and pictures and warmth. She felt betrayed, but it was her own fault. She should have told him her parents were dead or something.

"It's for your own good," he said, for what she swore must have been the tenth time. She wasn't really listening. "You're building up a poor image. The fan magazines are starting to get suspicious because they never see you with your parents."

She stared at him blankly, horrified.

He went on about how much her parents loved her, how worried they were about her. At last he broke down and told her the real reason. "And I'm worried, too," he said. "My conscience won't let me sleep some nights."

She couldn't remember ever hearing him plead before.

"Look, you just have to see them for a little while, for breakfast tomorrow, at the Stage Delicatessen. I'll pick you up and drive you there myself."

She laughed to think that tomorrow was Sunday. Even when she was a child, Sunday was the only day she ever ate breakfast, because her father was home, because they were a family. But she was so young then.

Bob took her smile for agreement and calmed down. He hugged her. That hug took all the strength to argue out of her.

He picked her up at nine o'clock the next morning. The white Cadillac pulled up in front of the delicatessen. She got out, or at least he opened the door for her. Sometimes she imagined her slow steps as she walked inside. Once she even took it as far as seeing her parents' anxious faces in the distance. She never let them come any closer.

𝄞 She was home alone when the phone rang. She was going to the doctor only once a week now, so she was usually home.

"Hey, Bruce. Fantastic, cuz. Where are you?"

Bruce was her fat cousin, the son of her mother's sister who died of cancer ten years ago. Bruce was twenty-four and lived mostly in Vegas, but he'd been in Atlantic City last summer pushing a rolling-chair during the tourist rush. She had barely known him until she ran into him on the street last summer and they got talking. In just a few weeks, she had gotten close enough to him that he understood how much she needed to get out of that town. He had escaped, hadn't he? It gave her courage. They'd been corresponding since he'd returned to Vegas, and he'd invited her out there.

"I'm in town," he said. "I wanted to see my kids."

"Hey, great. Do you want to come over?"

"Sure."

"Okay, I'll see you soon, then."

"Wait a minute, cuz," he said. "What are you going to wear?"

"What?"

"What are you going to wear for me?"

"Jeans."

"I want you to put on a dress for me."

"Why?"

"I just want you to, that's all."

"I don't understand."

"Look, I'll give it to you straight. If you come out to Vegas, you're going to have to work for me. I want to see how you look first."

"What are you talking about?"

"I'm talking about the streets, cuz."

"What streets?"

"Vegas streets, damn it. If you come out there, then you're going to have to work the streets for me, like my other girls."

"What?"

"How the hell do you think I get my money? Not pushing some dip-shit chair, that's for sure. Do you think I'm going to just support you?"

"I guess I didn't think about it."

"Well, think about it now. I'll call back tomorrow, and I'll expect some kind of answer."

The next day he didn't bother to call. Five days later, Janet, Bruce's estranged wife, phoned to see if she had Bruce's new address, because there was something she had to send him.

"But he's in town."

"What? Where?"

"He told me he was staying at your place."

"I haven't heard from him in over two months."

"What's going on here?"

She ended up telling Janet what was going on. Janet was as confused as she was about his phone call. He hadn't been in town, so he must have called from Vegas. Maybe he had gotten scared at the thought of her going out there and didn't have the nerve to say that, so this was his way of making sure she didn't go. He told her later that he never called. He said she'd imagined it.

𝄞 Tonight not pacing, spinning. Tonight she spoke to them, as they'd been wanting all along. Only the speech came out gibberish. She said she planned it that way, and she meant it. Grandma Shirley was here tonight.

Grandma Shirley was in the back bedroom, home from the nursing home because she'd insisted, even though the doctor said she was too sick to be moved. She couldn't leave that room, and she was getting all the attention.

Grandma Shirley was the only one they cared about. Earlier, her father interrupted her pacing to say she'd upset Grandma Shirley. Then he didn't understand what he said wrong. He didn't understand how much she needed her fantasy tonight. This was his house, and God damn it, he intended to live in it.

She sat in his kitchen chair and spun like a little girl. She wanted to be a child again. She didn't want to be a woman. God, she didn't want to ever be a woman, didn't want some man she thought was her friend to suddenly turn around and want her body. She didn't want a body. She wanted them all to leave her alone. They always let her down when she needed them.

All she needed was this chair to spin and this table to push off of – not to eat here, never to eat here, never again, never to eat again. To lose her body. At least then the doctors, maybe, would care for her.

But see how the doctors cared. Both the family physician and the psychologist came to watch her spin, plus Dr. Freed on the phone from Philadelphia. It was trick-or-treat time, the way as a child she bent over, put her head on the floor, and spun, first pushing around with the palms of her hands, then no hands and faster. She got a candy apple for that. She was their trick that night. And she was still their trick. She was only sixteen. She wasn't legal yet. Her parents could have had Bruce arrested if she'd gone out there.

The chair spun, and she spun in it. With a bent arm she pointed to the house next door, though the point kept moving as the chair turned. Over and over again she said, "*Er O, er O, er O.*" Her know. Well, Harriet *did* know. Harriet was the only person she could talk to, and she had to talk to someone. Even as a little girl, she always seemed to end up friendlier with the mothers of her friends than with the kids. Adults understood her – all adults except her parents, that is. Harriet understood why she could no longer go to school, had known for months that she was planning to run away, and knew Bruce had called her. Harriet kept her mouth shut behind her thick glasses, knew the Top Forty hits better than most of the kids, and sometimes, when the two of them were alone, even sang a little.

Her mother was close to Harriet. They had coffee together, and they went to the supermarket together. But her mother had no idea how close her daughter was to Harriet, even though she was sitting there pointing it out to them – *Er O, er*

O, *er* O, *er* O, *er* O – as if she were pleading with them to find out.

But the people in this house didn't really know her. In the next room she heard them discussing whether or not to put her in the hospital "just for the night." They assumed she was so sick that they didn't even whisper. "I'd like to give her a shot to calm her down," the doctor said. "But she'd have to be monitored closely. You couldn't keep her at home."

"Do you think it's that serious?" Her mother's continual question.

"I'm not sure how aware she is of what she's doing."

"It's also a problem that, once we get her in the hospital, we might not be able to release her too soon," the psychologist said. "It's liable to be fairly traumatic for her to be around that many people."

"I'm just not sure. And it's too late to call Dr. Freed again now."

It was time to put a stop to this. Calmly, silently, she went into her bedroom, closed the door, and went to sleep in her clothes, in case they came in the middle of the night to get her. Instead, the ambulance came to take Grandma Shirley back to the nursing home.

𝄞 Really she was pleading, desperate for someone to put a stop to all this, to take her in hand and make her face reality – whatever that was – make her go to school, maybe. Her parents never did. The psychiatrist never did. Certainly Uncle Steve would never do that, any more than Grandma Dora or Grandma Shirley would.

Bob pulled the car over to the curb and turned off the motor. He stared out the windshield. She knew what she was supposed to do now, and he knew she knew it. She was supposed to get out, enter the ABC Building, go up to the tenth floor, enter Dick's office, apologize to him, admit that he was right to tell Bob when he caught her drunk at a nightclub, that she didn't blame him, and that really she was grateful. Well, she wasn't. Bob had given her one hell of a slap across the face to get her into the car. His eyes, staring straight ahead like that, said he would do it again if he had to, right here in public. Touching the handle of the door was like picking up an ice cube, even with the sun beaming on it. It hurt her hand to pull it. But she did.

One foot in front of the other, she walked into the building, into the elevator, up to the tenth floor. At the office door, she paused. She could enter without knocking. All Dick's close friends could do that, and if he didn't want them to, if he was in a private conference, he simply locked the door to anyone and everyone, never making exceptions or excluding one friend in particular. But she didn't want to do it that way, not this time.

She walked two doors down, into the reception room. Marlene, Dick's secretary, knew her, of course, and even knew the say she liked her coffee. milk, two sugars. She didn't have to announce herself to her, but she did. And then, curtly: "Please tell Mr. Clark that I'd like to see him."

A quizzical look but no questions. She was announced, simply, briefly. A moment later "Mr. Clark" came out, his hand extended in a formal greeting, which caught her off-guard. She backed away, sighed, and then, almost in a whisper, as if she didn't have the courage to get up the words, she said, "Bob says I have to apologize."

"And what do *you* say?"

She bit her lower lip. Tears were welling up, and she was blinking. Damn it, she'd thought she was hardened. She bent her head and sighed again. "I'm sorry."

Dick's arm was around her in that confident gesture. He

guided her into his office, much as Dr. Freed did. There was only one door between Dick's office and the reception room, though. He didn't need the vestibule and double doors that Dr. Freed's office had, to make sure what was said in the office couldn't be overheard. Dick's office was spacious and modern, with white Formica chairs and clean fluffy cushions, a far cry from the stuffy antiques in Dr. Freed's cubbyhole.

Once inside the office, Dick hugged her, something Dr. Freed would never do. But she wasn't about to let him, or herself, off this easily. She wanted to talk about it, to work it out, to make him see her point of view, to admit she was foolish. She didn't know what.

"I guess I care more about your friendship than I realized," she said. "I really missed you." She was avoiding the issue, and she knew it. "Anyway, like Bob says, I guess you were doing it for my own good."

"You know I was." Dick had a reserve that kept him on top of any situation. Usually she envied it, but right now she hated him for it. She wanted some response, damn it, wanted him to get as emotional as she was. But he wouldn't. Couldn't. His damn WASP background. All he said was "Don't forget, I've got a vested interest in all you kids I knew from the start."

"Okay, just don't rub it in, all right? I said I was sorry."

Even that Dick took calmly. He sat there silent, waiting, knowing she'd back down in a minute.

Sure enough, a moment later she broke down and smiled, about to start crying again, from relief this time. It had been a long, hard month, avoiding him, avoiding certain restaurants, driving past Frankie's and not stopping when she saw Dick's car there, wondering if they were discussing her. At the same time, she never doubted for a moment that it would all pass.

They talked on, like old times. Neither of them mentioned

her phone call at midnight, when she told him off and hung up. Dick knew her well enough to know she didn't mean it, so even then he hadn't reacted.

It was forty-five minutes later when she remembered Bob sitting out in the car. She dashed out and said it was all okay, as if he couldn't tell by the sight of her. She asked him to join them, but he had to get back to the office. Dick would drive her home. She didn't even ask. She knew he would.

And here she was, sitting on the front seat of a new large car again. Dick's car this time. No, her father's Chrysler. It was parked outside Grandma Dora's. And here she was, crying. What had happened in the ten miles since they'd left the house? Probably some comment her father had made, like asking her to comb her hair back, trying to control her, being ashamed of her.

That did it. She didn't care that the whole family was going over to Grandma Dora's to see her father's cousin Bill, in town from California. It wasn't her family, anyway, not in the real sense. She'd be damned if she was going to get out of that car. She'd wait for them here.

A tap on the window. Uncle Steve. She opened the door for him, and he knelt down and put his arm around her. "Aren't you going to come up and see Bill?" he asked. "He's my baby cousin."

"No."

"Please."

"I don't want to see anyone."

"Bill came all the way from California just to see us."

"I don't care. Leave me alone." It was the first time she'd ever said that to Uncle Steve. Usually she was desperate for his attention.

"Please. Come in for my sake."

"No." Weaker this time.

He took out his handkerchief and started to wipe away her tears. "You don't have to stay long," he said. "Just come in for a few minutes and say hello."

"No. Please."

"Bill will be hurt if you don't come in. Grandma Dora will be hurt."

"Just leave me alone."

"Come in for my sake. I'll be hurt if you don't come in."

"I just want to sit out here."

"It's cold out here. Look, I didn't even put my jacket on. You don't want me to freeze, do you?"

"I'll be okay out here."

"Come in for my sake. You've never met my baby cousin. Bill's the one I was closest to."

"I don't want to see people."

"Everyone wants to see you."

"No, they don't."

"Don't be silly. Bill was saying how much he was looking forward to meeting you."

"Really?"

"Cross my heart. Please. Just for a few minutes." He was wiping her tears again. Then he took her hand, gently, tentatively, to lead her out. In.

Then the moment she got restless, her parents took her home. No one had made her toe the line – not now, not ever – but they'd gotten her to go for it like a baby whose attention you divert, to get his mouth open and shove the food in. She'd hardly known what was happening to her.

CHAPTER SIX

December 1966 – May 1969
Ages eighteen to twenty

Songs in the Top Forty included
I'M A BELIEVER
TO SIR WITH LOVE
ODE TO BILLY JOE
MRS. ROBINSON
I HEARD IT THROUGH THE GRAPEVINE

IT WAS CHRISTMAS EVE, AND first thing that morning she had flunked her driving test. She hung around her father's office for a while and then got one of the men who worked for him to drive her home. As she entered the empty house, she had no idea what she was really thinking. It wasn't until she had been alone a while, until the walls started closing in on her, that she realized how alone she was.

She made a bet with herself: the Ben Casey rerun would be on in a few minutes. If it was a program she hadn't seen before, she would watch it and see how she felt afterward. If it was a story she already knew, then she'd kill herself. It was the old working-on-Christmas rerun.

She'd been saving the pills, four or five out of every bottle over the past three years, but she never knew for what or why or when or how. She must have had a hundred pills saved up. And there was also the liquor her father kept for company. She'd heard it added to the effect of tranquilizers. A hundred pills, an eight-ounce glass of Scotch – she didn't bother to put ice in. After that, she undressed and went to bed.

She woke up maybe three hours later, and she wasn't dead yet. She called the neighbor she always called. "Harriet, you know where the key is. Come in."

"What's wrong?"

She didn't say anything. Harriet came in. She saw the empty bottle of pills and smelled the liquor.

"I'll call the woman taking care of my mother. She's a nurse." She also called an ambulance. The nurse stuck a finger down her throat to make her vomit, and so she avoided having her stomach pumped. The last thing she recalled before falling asleep again was Harriet phoning her father's office. From across the room she could hear her mother shriek into the phone, "I was afraid something like this would happen."

"You got off easy," her parents told her. She was in the hospital only five days. If Dr. Freed hadn't called long-distance to satisfy the hospital staff that she was indeed under his treatment, they would have put her through all sorts of psychiatric tests. They probably would have shipped her off to the nearest mental institution, in Egg Harbor, forty miles away. They would have, at least, moved her to the psychiatric ward, if Dr. Freed hadn't vouched for her and signed papers to release her as soon as she was physically able. She ought to be grateful.

She was grateful that Dr. Freed gave her another prescription for sleeping pills, pills that wouldn't react with the pills she'd swallowed, so she could get some sleep. He didn't press her for details about what had happened. He knew she would talk when she was ready.

𝄞 She took driving lessons from a real teacher this time, and she got her license. Her father bought her a used Chevy, only three years old and with low mileage. At last she felt she could do almost anything.

"I'll be perfectly fine," she said.

"You're on all those tranquilizers. You have no idea what you're doing half the time." Her father was about to turn his back on her.

"I know perfectly well what I'm doing. I've been on those drugs so long they don't affect me any more."

"Then why do you still fall down in the middle of the night? How do you think your mother and I feel, wakened out of a deep sleep by a loud crash because you got up to go to the bathroom?"

"That only happens at night."

"One of these nights, you're going to kill yourself."

"So I'll kill myself. You won't have to worry about me driving to Philly any more."

"You're not driving there, and that's final."

"Okay, then I won't go to the doctor."

"I don't understand why you don't want to take the bus," her mother said, half a question.

"You don't understand anything." They didn't understand because she hadn't told them. How could she tell them that the other people on the bus spoke to her now? The men sounded like her cousin Bruce. She was afraid of them. She was afraid one of these days she might find herself going off with one of them. "You just don't understand," she said again.

"I understand that I have to go to work at six o'clock in the morning," her father said. "I can't afford to go get you in the middle of the night because you cracked up the car somewhere. I'm not as young as I used to be."

"I haven't done that for months," she said. "I'm in control now."

"You're crazy."

"That's right, I am. And you're the ones who made me this way, remember?"

Her father stomped out of the room. "It's useless trying to talk to her. Let her go. Let her crack up the car. Let her kill herself. I don't care any more."

A moment later she heard the TV, loud.

"I really don't think you ought to drive," her mother ventured.

"Well, I'm driving anyway." She walked off into her room and shut the door.

The next morning she drove up to Philly without even getting a speeding ticket. She parked in an outside lot so she wouldn't dent the front fender leaving the inside lot, the way she had a few weeks ago. She went off to the record stores. She had over two hours to kill.

She was finished half an hour early, laden down with a stack of albums that had been on sale – Pat Boone, the Everly Brothers, Johnny Horton, Simon and Garfunkel, Connie Francis, Bobby Vee, Jimmy Clanton, Bobby Vinton – records she would listen to once and then put away. She decided to drop them off in the car before she went to the doctor's. Slowly, in control, she asked the attendant if she could put them in her car, and he said yes, as if she were a normal person. She put them in the trunk and slammed it shut. The keys were locked in there, tangled in the handle of the shopping bag.

She'd left the ignition in OFF, rather than LOCK, so she could drive home. That night her father took the back seat apart to get into the trunk, while she stood there watching as if her hands were tied. But at least this time she hadn't panicked. She'd controlled herself.

𝄞 She had begun to trust doctors. Doctors guarded her fantasies. They tried to become a bridge between her and her parents, but she didn't have to cross if she didn't want to. She didn't have to do anything she didn't want. The doctors saw to that. Not all of them were out to get her.

Then she went to see the movie *The Young Doctors*. It was made in 1961, but she'd somehow missed seeing it then, even though Dick had starred in it. On a rainy day in Philly, when she had a few hours to kill, it happened to be playing at the Fulton, two blocks from Dr. Freed's office. Despite the movie's title, it had never dawned on her that Dick would play a doctor. He played an intern or resident and looked really good in white.

Seeing the movie confused her. She wanted the real world to go along with her fantasies and feed new situations to her imagination. But after she saw *The Young Doctors*, the people in her fantasies started switching places with people in the real world. She had always worked carefully to keep them separate. She watched Ben Casey and Dr. Kildare and for an hour put herself in the place of the patient, but she was very careful not to imagine knowing those doctors in real life. Now the real world had tricked her.

She supposed there was a correlation. In her fantasies Dick was always helping her, helping everyone. He was a father or big-brother figure. She could make him pursue a more substantial career now. She could pretend the doctor role was played by another actor, or she could keep him playing the role and go through a scene about what it felt like to portray a doctor. No, no, she couldn't. She tried the fantasy in every direction, but none of them seemed right. At the end of the movie, Dick's girlfriend, who was ice-skating in one of the early scenes, had her leg amputated. But he married her anyway. Maybe that was proof that Dick would like her the way she was. They'd take it step by step, and she too would recover.

What made her think she had to change the fantasies just because she'd seen some stupid movie? For a while she would concentrate on fantasies Dick didn't appear in and keep him at a safe distance, as at first she had done with real doctors.

Even so, she missed him. Why the hell did it have to be a doctor? Anything else she could have dealt with: have him talk about playing the role, maybe with her playing opposite. But not this, not this. She looked in Dr. Freed's eyes and saw Dick maybe thirty years from now. And for the first time she realized she no longer wanted to be a patient. But how could she tell Dr. Freed? She no longer wanted to talk to him at all.

𝄞 Her fantasies had fallen apart on her once before, and she'd gotten them back again. It was Dick's fault that time, too. Suddenly it was 1960 all over again. The word *payola* echoed in her mind. *Payola*: taking money for publicizing or pushing a particular singer or record, bribery, kickback, an illegal practice.

She remembered how she'd stared at the front page of the *Philadelphia Bulletin* while her father read the middle of the paper. The moment he walked away, she laid the section flat on the floor, kneeling before it, at first simply staring, letting herself digest the headline for a moment before reading further:

DICK CLARK AND OTHER AREA DISK JOCKEYS ACCUSED OF PAYOLA.

Slowly she read the article on page one, then on page eight. She would need no fan magazines for the next two weeks. Next morning, the *Atlantic City Press* carried the Associated Press version. The *Bulletin*, Dick's hometown paper, did its own research: comments from area singers, regulars who appeared on the show, photos. Thank God, both Frankie and Bobby refused to comment, and all Fabe said was that, if this was the practice, he'd never been aware of it. After the first few articles on "area disk jockeys," the journalists wrote only about Dick, making him the scapegoat.

She was afraid they'd cancel *Bandstand*, but it had its biggest audience ever. She remembered being eight years old and watching Grandma Dora turn on the *Tonight* show and wait on the edge of her chair to see if Jack Paar would walk off again, as he'd done a few nights before. But Dick was too considerate, and, scapegoat or not, he had no way of escaping.

By the time she'd finished reading the first article, she was convinced that Dick wasn't guilty and had nothing to run from. But even the reporters supposedly giving Dick's point of view seemed to convict him. She wished at least one reporter would tell the real story. Probably they couldn't, though, or they'd lose their jobs. Parents wanted scandal to throw in the faces of their children who skipped their homework to watch *Bandstand* and listen to these singers who couldn't sing. It was the parents who bought the papers and who would be sitting on that court bench. She didn't think Dick had a chance.

She knew all about false charges. People were sent to prison for crimes they didn't commit. A huge case was made out of a tiny incident that with any other person would be overlooked. Her cousin Bruce had spent a year in jail for "selling alcoholic beverages to minors," and he'd told her all about it. Sure, Dick had probably taken a few kickbacks. If he hadn't, he wouldn't be human. If Dick *did* go to prison, he'd get special treatment. They'd respect the fact that he was a star, and no one would dare harm him. It wouldn't be like Bruce getting his arm broken in a prison fight. But she had no intention of letting him go to prison, and for once the real world agreed with her fantasy.

How had she handled the fantasy then, seven years ago? Frankie, Paul, Bobby, Annette – all his friends came out against him, finding him guilty in their private conversations, though on principle they refused to testify. She had been the only one to stick up for him, even though it meant speaking out against the others. She took the chance of losing their friendships, which in the end she didn't lose. She proved to Dick she was a good friend, and she agreed to appear on his show when no one else would.

Then she turned it the other way: she spoke out against Dick. She stuck up for what was right, even though he had helped her get her start, even though she risked losing friendships. He thanked her in the end. In his heart he knew he'd been wrong. Of course, he was grateful she didn't testify, so there was no real harm done.

In one fantasy she took the easy way out and had them all stick by Dick: her, Frankie, Fabe, Bobby, Paul, everyone. That way she didn't have to set anyone apart from the group. People discussed their doubts. They consoled and supported one another, sticking together as always – one big happy family. After all, how could someone she knew do anything wrong, someone who understood her so well, someone she looked up to?

𝄞 The payola scandal. *The Young Doctors*. The fantasies were losing their power. Often she found herself pacing the living room with nothing in her mind, pacing simply because it was expected of her or she expected it of herself. The fantasies, when they came, grew shorter and shorter, and they didn't always end happily. She found herself eating less and less. Her weight went down to ninety pounds. Now that her own world no longer made claims on her energy, there was no reason to bother eating.

She couldn't take her eyes off Frankie's white shoes: not a single scuff mark. He tapped his right foot gently as he talked, in rhythm with his thoughts. What she wouldn't have given, as a child, to have had white loafers like that or white oxfords, even brown and white or black and white. But no, her shoes were always all black or all brown. One time in second grade they bought her white bucks with soft crepe soles. She was in heaven. She watched where she was going, walking to school one foot in front of the other, careful not to scrape them on the ground, cautious at the curbs to step high enough, trying to be light on her feet and not wear down the heels right away, as her parents said she would. All morning she kept them neatly beneath her desk, feet firmly on the floor, never crossing her legs. At eleven o'clock, as they lined up to go out for recess, Sherry – big fat Sherry, who two weeks ago had tried to take a ball away from her and swore she'd get her back after she told the teacher and fixed it so Sherry had to stay after school – Sherry lined up in front of her and, when the line started moving, backed up hard as if she'd been pushed, her heels aimed directly at the smooth white toes, smudging them.

Frankie's foot beat perfect time. Even as a child, he must have been sure of himself. No one ever pushed him around, even though he was small for his age. She might be famous now, but nothing had really changed. If she wore white shoes, she would probably scuff them.

CHAPTER SEVEN

June – August 1969
Age twenty

Songs in the Top Forty included
GET BACK
LOVE THEME FROM ROMEO AND JULIET
IN THE YEAR 2525
HONKY TONK WOMEN

"CAN YOU BELIEVE IT – I didn't even want to get out of the car to meet you?" she laughed.

Bill didn't answer, just smiled that smile she'd come to adore. He was an amazing cross between her father and Uncle Steve – with all of Uncle Steve's charm but with her father's laid-back, quiet quality. His deep blue eyes seemed to understand, without him having to make a show of all he was doing for her.

She followed him up the steps to the house he'd talked about often, the house he'd designed himself. The living room, a different shape from her parents', had built-in sofas along the front and left walls, a coffee table joining them, and a built-in stereo, which with its top closed could be another coffee table. The piano was alongside that. The dining room, off to the side, had no door but was a separate room. There was a sort of picnic table, painted the same light color as the living-room furniture: it looked almost like imitation wood.

Now the whole neighborhood would see if she paced. The front of the room was glass, and the side was glass opening out on a patio. Anyway, this was the real California. This was her father's cousin Bill. His daughter, Lesley, was her age and accepted her in a way no one in Atlantic City had. That first day, she was permitted to ride in the front seat of Lesley's small green convertible while she and her boyfriend, Seth, drove her around and showed her the mountains going right to the sea. A good place to jump from, she noted. Just in case.

People who live in glass houses shouldn't throw stones. And people who sit under trees should be careful of falling fruit. As Lesley, Seth, and she sat under the peach tree, as the smoke filled her lungs because she was inhaling despite their warnings, she counted off the possibilities in her mind: where the fruit would hit if it fell and how people too could hit her.

"This sure is great grass," Lesley said.

"You bet." Seth looked straight up at heaven.

"Not as good as ours would have been, though. I still don't believe that deer."

"Really."

Lesley turned to her. "We've been trying to grow some grass up in the mountains, only a deer's been eating it."

"That must be one happy deer," Seth said.

"Really."

"We've got to catch that deer."

"Really."

"Can you picture how great that grass would have been?"

"Really."

"We've got to catch that deer."

"I'd like to hang him upside down by his hooves," Lesley said. "To scare off any other deer that might get bright ideas."

"Like a scarecrow."

"An upside-down scarecrow."

"That would teach him."

"Really."

"Then we could roast him," Seth said. "Have you ever eaten venison?"

"No," Lesley said.

"It's even more tender than steak is."

"Great. That would teach him."

"You bet."

"We could invite everyone over."

"We'd probably get stoned from all the grass in his bloodstream," Seth added.

"Really."

"All that great grass."

"Sure would like to catch that deer."

"We've really got to catch that deer."

She was sure they were talking about her and what they would do to her if she told Lesley's parents that they got her stoned. She inhaled again. She grew more and more frightened. She wasn't going to fit in, after all.

Lesley's mother came home, then Bill. She must brace herself, try to walk a straight line, speak to them. She must remember to chew her food. She must remember to swallow. The glass house was all around her. At last excused, she made it step by step into the living room, to the far corner of the sofa, by the stereo, behind the piano. Lesley put on an Engelbert Humperdinck record. The deep sound of the bass went in her left ear, pounded in her head, exited. Everything slowed down. She heard it note by note. For the first time ever, she could hear the rhythm.

And after the rhythm, weeks after, other things entered her head: words, thoughts, feelings. The words in particular weren't always what she was expecting—words like *pretentious*. Lesley said she liked the kids from San Fernando Valley, rather than those from Beverly Hills and Hollywood Hills, because they were less pretentious.

"We don't wear bras or makeup, and we drive Volkswagens and Mustangs, not Jaguars or Cadillacs."

"What's wrong with Cadillacs and makeup?"

"It's pretentious. Those kids are always trying to be what they're not. They're putting on false fronts, and it's the same in their friendships."

"I don't understand."

"Look, you like hanging out with me and Seth and our friends, right?"

"Sure." She would have liked hanging out with anyone, anyone who was willing to be her friend. She thought Lesley understood that. No one had been this accepting of her since she was three years old and Richard used to follow her around the house.

"Well, it's because we're easy to be with," Lesley said. "We're straight with people. We accept people the way they are."

"If we don't like someone or something, we say so," Seth added. "You don't have to worry about what we're saying behind your back."

"Right. And we're honest. We don't pretend to like someone or something just to go along with the crowd."

They could have been describing the kids in Atlantic City, only worse. "Are they really that bad? All of them?"

"I went through grammar school with those kids," Lesley said. "They were my friends for a while. At least, I thought they were. Growing up in this neighborhood and all, I had no choice. That's why my parents built this house here. They wanted me to be friendly with all the rich kids. They never stopped to think that I wouldn't fit in. But how do you think it felt when I wasn't invited to some of their parties, like at the country club, because I wasn't rich enough?"

"Did that really happen?'"

"Sure it did. Eight years old and they had birthday parties at the country club. I was ashamed to even have a birthday party. It would have to be at home, and I was afraid the kids would make fun of me if they saw how small my house was and that we didn't have a swimming pool. It got worse as I got older."

"But you have so many friends."

"I didn't used to, not until I got to high school and had more kids to choose from, more of my own kind."

She curled back against the pillow Lesley had tossed to the bottom of the bed. It was late. She knew Lesley and Seth had smoked a lot of hash and wanted to lie back and enjoy it now. But she had to know – not about what Lesley and her friends were like but about the others, the children, the brothers and sisters of the movie stars: Annette, with her giant pool and two younger brothers, and Shelley. "They couldn't have really been that way, not all of them. What about the children of the movie stars?"

"They were even worse. God, those kids were so stuck up you wouldn't believe it."

"All of them?"

"All of them. Oh, dahrling, I just loooove your new pink pahrty dress. The color makes your eyes just sparkle so. Really, it's just deevine." Lesley's voice rose an octave. She and Seth couldn't stop laughing. "Then, of course, the minute you walk away, they're whispering about how fat you look. I could never afford clothes that were as good as theirs, either. God, half of them had their school outfits custom-made."

"I don't believe it."

"Well, you better start believing it. I mean, dahrling, I just wouldn't, couldn't lie, not to someone as intelligent as you ahre." She pointed with her little finger for emphasis. She and Seth cracked up again.

"But there must be some mistake. I mean, maybe the kids were like that. I know how awful kids can be. But what about their parents? Most of them must have been poor before they were stars and all. They wouldn't forget that easily."

"Where do you think the kids learned it from? I remember once, when I was about seven, I went to a pool party at Bing Crosby's daughter's house, and her mother took pity on me and gave me all these dresses her older daughter had outgrown. I was never so embarrassed. And wouldn't you know it? My mother was just delighted. She kept on saying all week how lucky we were."

"That's awful."

"Then when I was in fourth grade, I got close with Dean Martin's daughter. I invited her over on a Saturday, and we had a really good time. At least, I thought we did. But then in school on Monday she was telling all the kids how dilapidated my house was. She said she'd told her parents all about it and they told her never to play with me again. It was terrible. Another woman told her daughter to stay away from me because I was over there playing and when my mother came to pick me up, she was driving a Chevy."

"What did your parents say?"

"I never told them. They wouldn't have understood, anyway."

"Stop and think about it," Seth cut in. Seth was studying philosophy, like nearly everyone in California. "The movie stars are in front of cameras all day long, day after day. Their whole lives are a public spectacle. How can they help but be acting all the time, in real life too? You can't blame them, really. I'm sure a lot of them don't intend to be that way. They just can't help themselves."

She said good night and went into her room. She was sure Lesley and Seth were glad to be alone. She liked Seth and Lesley, and she liked their friends. They'd accepted her, no questions asked. She'd known all along that what they said was true. She'd been deceiving herself, believing in idols she had no chance of meeting. They'd never step out from their photographs, never go to the same school with her, never be close enough for her to see what they were really like. So they could never do what Arlene did: abandon her on a street corner when she wasn't allowed to cross the street herself and didn't know how to walk home alone. They could never leave her standing there with some stupid doll she didn't even like and didn't know what to do with when Arlene went off to play with some other friend. No one would ever do that to her again.

𝄞 For almost a week she'd gotten only two hours' sleep a night. With luck maybe the cameras would pick up nothing but the black circles under her eyes. Maybe the album would sell on the strength of her desperate need for someone to take care of her. But that wasn't the image Bob and Pete wanted to put across.

"Remember how nervous you were before you cut the album," Pete said. "That worked out just fine, didn't it? You sang better than you ever did. Well, you know we won't let you down this time either." Pete's arm was around her. More than once, she'd suspected Pete wanted more than just to comfort her, but he held his fingers perfectly still and steady now. Seeing them together, a stranger might assume he was her father.

That was what she feared: that she would discover her father was behind that camera. Her father never, ever, made her look good in pictures, and then he blamed her for not being photogenic. Her father's pictures made her mother look old and drawn because he took forever to line up the shot. Her father, with light meters and zoom lenses and wide-angle lenses and three different kinds of flash, took pictures that looked like Kodak snapshots. She vowed never to pose for him again.

Neither Bob nor Pete had any idea how much they were asking. How could she tell them? They'd only laugh at her. They'd say this was different. They'd remind her that she always knew that if her singles sold, they'd want her to cut an album, and the sales of an album depended as much on the cover photo as on the music. She just hadn't expected the day would ever come. She never really thought she'd be famous. But she wasn't famous enough, not yet. At least they weren't planning a portfolio of pictures inside the album, as they'd done with Frankie and Fabe. They'd take thirty, forty, maybe fifty poses, and all they needed was one.

They tried to make it as easy as possible by having the photographer come to her home. She couldn't bring herself to tell them she'd be more comfortable in the strangeness of the studio. She never wanted to let her father inside her house again. Instead, she'd count to ten, say cheese, and hope for the best. Maybe she could smile like her mother in her wedding portrait, the one and only time she was beautiful.

That morning Bob and Pete arrived first, with the makeup crew on their heels. Then the lighting technicians and the prop men came. The photographer was the last to show up. All he did was place her where he wanted her, brush back a hair or two, ask her to make her smile a little bigger or smaller, to tilt her head this way or that. That was all there was to it. Tomorrow she would be forced to look at the pictures.

She walked into Bob's office and she looked past him to a six-inch pile of photos on his desk. He made her sit down. He made her wait while he poured her a Diet Pepsi and vodka and tonic for himself and Pete. Even his speech was slow today. At last she heard him saying they'd pretty much decided. He handed her the photo. Her pearl pendant gleamed in the lower center of the picture. Her head tilted toward the imagined lover or buyer, as if she idolized his every word. Her eyes danced. She understood why they'd chosen this one.

She closed her eyes to block out what she didn't want to see. As her eyelids pounded, she realized what was frightening her. My God, she looked exactly like Arlene.

CHAPTER EIGHT

September 1969 – March 1970
Ages twenty and twenty-one

Songs in the Top Forty included
LEAVING ON A JET PLANE
RAINDROPS KEEP FALLING ON MY HEAD
BRIDGE OVER TROUBLED WATER

ALL OF A SUDDEN SHE WAS glad she wasn't famous. Not being famous meant she could be anything she wanted. She didn't even have to live in California. She could live in New York, for example.

She closed her eyes and imagined the plane landing in New York instead of Philadelphia. Her parents wouldn't be meeting her. She'd take a cab to a hotel, and the next day she'd look for an apartment. Or she'd look for work first. She had good typing skills, and she could learn shorthand. She'd always been a quick learner when she put her mind to something. One thing she had going for her was that she was stubborn. She'd learned at least that much about herself after all her years of seeing a psychiatrist.

She had to get out of California. She had to start fresh, away from relatives, away from anyone who knew her family, if she was going to build a life of her own. The only place she could do that was a large city like New York, where there were all sorts of people and you could walk the streets without everyone knowing you. She'd take her chances on getting mugged. Only she had to go home first, at least for a week or two. Bill had warned her to ease her parents into the idea that she could live alone now. It wasn't going to be easy for them, either, he had said. They were used to her being sick and fragile.

𝄞 Her room seemed so small. Had she really locked herself in here day after day? Everything in it felt alien now: the dresser with all the clothes crammed into one drawer, the fan magazines that filled the other drawers, the old record player, the recliner with the reading light hung above it. Had she really ever been happy here?

She knew she'd have no trouble convincing her parents to help her get started in New York. After all, they'd paid for the trip to California – anything to make her happy. If they thought she was about to break down again, if she pretended maybe to get sick, hibernate, hide, they'd try anything. But how long was she going to keep doing this?

She picked up a magazine and glanced at pictures from a slumber party at Annette's, but somehow she couldn't get interested in Annette saying it cost only two dollars a person for all the food. How could anyone believe the expense mattered to her? She knew better now. She tried another magazine and another. Each was worse than the one before.

Then she thought of Harriet. Ever since Dave had gone off to college, Harriet had been working part-time in the candy store four blocks away. They used to talk for hours about the stars when she bought the magazines. Harriet never acted as if she were sick or anything. Maybe she would understand what she still wasn't sure how to tell her parents: that these magazines were locking her in that room, and she felt strong enough to go out now.

Carefully, one by one, she filled a shopping bag with magazines, at first looking them over for any she wanted to save, then not even bothering with that. She filled four bags and still had magazines left. She carried two bags at a time out to the car.

"What am I going to do with these?" Harriet asked her when she walked into the candy store.

"You could sell them. Lots of people still want these magazines."

"We don't sell used magazines."

"They're in good condition. Some of them aren't that old yet. And they're good ones. You know how carefully I always chose them."

"I can't do anything with them."

"You don't have to give me a lot for them. I just have to offer my parents some of the money back. I'll give them to you for ten dollars a bag. Five dollars a bag. Even if you sold them for a dime apiece, you'd make that much back."

"I really don't think I can sell them. And I don't have room for them on the racks. The boss is liable to get mad if he sees them there. I don't own this place, remember."

"Just try it for a while and see if they sell. They will. I know they will. If not, I'll give you your money back. Please, I have to show my parents I don't need them any more."

At last Harriet agreed. "I'll keep them for two weeks. If they aren't selling by then, you'll have to take them back."

"That's great. Thanks a million." Her parents would see she was making the effort. This ought to prove she was well enough.

Her mother didn't want the twenty dollars. "The magazines are yours," she said. "We don't care about the money. We just want you to be happy. That's all that matters." It was useless trying to talk to her.

Harriet hadn't put any out on the racks. "I knew you'd be back for them," she said. "I wouldn't have done this for anyone else, mind you."

She gave her back the money. She picked out three of the most recent magazines and insisted Harriet keep them, for all her trouble. Her mother carried them out to the car for her, because she was feeling nauseous.

A few nights later she tried again. "Maybe we ought to give the magazines to the Children's Seashore Home?" she offered. "There's no reason for you to keep them around when I'm not here."

"Are you planning on going back to California?" her mother asked. "Bill mentioned you might decide to stay there, but he hasn't spoken of it in weeks, so I assumed he gave up the idea."

"I was thinking more about New York."

"What?" Two voices in unison.

"New York." A long, hollow pause. "There's really nothing for me to do in Atlantic City. I thought I'd try New York."

"Do you have any idea what apartments cost there?"

"Jobs pay more, too."

"Don't be ridiculous," her mother said. "You haven't worked since you were sixteen."

"That doesn't mean I can't work."

"Let Daddy speak to some of his friends, then. Maybe someone will have a job for you."

"I don't want a favor from any of Daddy's friends."

"You don't want anything we have to offer, do you? Living off in your fantasies as if we're not even in the house."

"You're right. I don't want anything to do with you." She

went into her room and closed the door but didn't slam it. They hadn't even noticed she'd been home four days and never once paced the living room.

She had nearly four hundred dollars in the bank from when she was sixteen and typing envelopes, four years ago. That was enough to get started. She would take a few days to work things out in her head. Then she would drive to New York. No, she'd take a bus. She wouldn't need a car there, as she did in Atlantic City or Los Angeles. A car would only be a hindrance.

She laughed, remembering a story Bill had told her. At eighteen, he'd been so desperate to leave home that he just left a note for his parents and hitched west.

"Don't let them trap you, kid," he had said. "There's no reason they have to trap you there."

𝄞 She convinced her parents to let her go to New York for two or three days. She could always come home if it didn't work out. They drove her to the bus station on Monday, and she was on her way. She got a room at the Martha Washington Hotel for Women, which sounded safe, for thirty dollars a week. She paid for two weeks in advance. Her parents didn't suspect that she'd closed her bank account. She bought a five-day-old *Village Voice* and started looking for a job, but she quickly discovered the decent jobs were already filled. So she had all day Tuesday to rest. She'd start early on Wednesday. She lay on the sagging mattress and ran her fingers over an imaginary typewriter keyboard. By her second try, she remembered where every letter was. She lay there practicing for an hour, making up words and typing them in her mind, till she got her fingers moving faster and faster.

She went to six interviews, and by Friday morning she had

a job as a clerk-typist at a mail-order place that sold Christmas decorations. Three dollars an hour sounded like a fortune. Finding a place to live was harder, but after four weeks of looking, a realtor found her a studio on First Avenue and Seventh Street.

𝄞 Over the past six years, even in her worst moments, there had been a ray of hope. Or a threat, depending on how you thought of it. She had told her parents, Harriet, Uncle Steve, Bruce, Richard, and herself, "If I live to be eighteen, it will be a miracle. If I make it to twenty-one, I'll be okay." She could will herself into health, once she decided to. She'd been living in New York for seven months and in California for two months before that: nine months of living in the real world, the time it takes for a fetus to form, the child she'd sworn she'd never have, not even now, not even though she was happy now. Her parents still treated her like a child. They had assumed she'd go back to Atlantic City in a week, two at the most. Her car was rusting in their driveway. If they didn't sell it soon, it wasn't going to be worth much.

She was as surprised as her family was. She was no longer afraid of people. The days of coming home and choking, of vomiting until the blood vessels in her face seemed to break from sheer tension, were over. She was holding onto her job. In January she'd enrolled in a sculpture class at N.Y.U. And she had made three friends. Sally was a woman she worked with who was also an actress and had gorgeous, wild red hair. After listening to one of Sally's monologues for ten minutes, she could never keep from laughing, no matter how depressed she might be. Martha, who lived in her building, was a painter who had been included in a few group shows. Just having

Martha close to her, working all the time, sparked a new dedication and interest. And Bob, whom she'd met through Sally, was tall, with longish brown hair and glasses. He was very masculine but also very gentle. He was an intern on *The Village Voice* while he was getting his M.F.A. from the Columbia Writing Program. These weren't friends her mother had tried to buy for her.

Except the bad habits of her past, when she paid no attention to her body, were catching up with her. She'd been to doctors during the past six years, and she'd accepted them. But dentists were different. Since the day she'd quit school, she hadn't set foot in a dentist's office. A tooth that had developed a cavity four years ago had grown severely infected. Her gum became so swollen that she couldn't even sleep on her left side. And people could see it. She couldn't convince herself she was faking this time. The tooth was loose and hurt like hell. She'd known for months that it had to be extracted.

She called her parents Thursday night as soon as she got home from work, instead of waiting until eleven o'clock, when the phone rates went down. "Does our medical insurance cover dentist bills?" she asked, trying to sound casual. Eventually she would get her own insurance where she worked, but her father's business provided extremely good coverage in the meantime.

"What's wrong?" her mother shrieked.

"One of my teeth is a mess. I guess I've been sort of letting it go. It has to be pulled now."

"Are you sure?"

"Of course I'm sure."

"I'll make an appointment with Dr. Sherman. When do you want to come in?"

"That's okay. I found a dentist up here."

"Dr. Sherman knows you. He'll understand how scared you are of pain. He's always been extremely gentle with you."

"I can't take that much time off work. It's easier to go to someone here."

"Dr. Sherman's pulled your teeth before. He knows the needle worries you more than the extraction. He'll give you gas, like last time. Most dentists won't take the time for that."

"Dr. Michelson already agreed to give me gas."

"You spoke to him already?"

"I made an appointment for a week from Saturday."

"You don't know anything about this guy."

"Bob recommended him."

"Who's Bob?"

"A friend." It slipped out before she realized. Now her parents would probably assume she was sleeping with him. They had no conception of the fact that men and women could simply be friends. That didn't happen in Atlantic City, at least as far as she could see. All that town understood was marriage. That was one of the reasons she was so much happier here. New York was a world her parents had no knowledge of. To them it was no different from her fantasy world.

After a long silence her mother recovered. "What time's your appointment? I'll take the bus up and go with you."

"That's not necessary."

"Don't be ridiculous. You're going to be knocked out and in pain. I don't even think they'll let you go home alone."

"My friend Sally said she'd go with me." Another long silence. In its reverberations she could hear her mother feeling rejected, useless, no longer needed. For the first time in years, she could relate to a feeling of her mother's. If it had been anyone but her mother, she might have relented.

𝄞 She was shaking when she put down the phone. And she was shaking a week from Saturday.

The appointment was for ten o'clock. It would take about two hours, including resting time in the recovery room afterward. Sally had said she'd pick her up at noon. There was nothing to be afraid of. She didn't know whether she was more worried about the pain or the thought that Sally might not be there. Maybe she should have let her mother come up, after all. No, Sally would be there, Sally would be there, Sally would be there.

She found herself saying, "Sally will be there," under her breath when the doctor told her to count backward from ten. She was breathing deeply. Sally will be there, Sally will... Sally. She heard someone else counting.

She felt a strong, confident hand remove the mask, as if patting her on the shoulder for a job well done. Dick's arm was around her. See, her friends would always be there when she needed them. She reached up to cuddle the arm, but it moved quickly across her chest and slapped her hand down. Now she felt it pinching her, hard. She tried to cry out that it hurt. "Dick, I apologized. I apologized just like Bob told me to." But her voice was muffled. Why was Dick doing this? Even when her father interrupted, her fantasy was never this bad.

She felt Dick tug her into his office. She didn't want to go. "You used us," he whispered in her ear—a shrill, piercing whisper. His finger was poking at her chest. He said it over and over, nailing her to the chair opposite his desk. Suddenly the chair was too small for her. She couldn't move in it. She would have apologized a hundred times, but she wasn't sure what she'd done wrong this time.

"You used us," Frankie shouted in her other ear. The smell of his cologne made her nauseous, like the perfume the kids had worn in high school. She hadn't realized how tall he was.

"You used us," Bob said, standing directly in front of her, one foot up on the footrest of her chair. His face was hard and suddenly lined with age. She told herself he was drunk or something, but she knew he wasn't. Even her father had never seemed so old or so angry. She wished she'd stayed home, where she belonged.

She wasn't like Donna. She wasn't like Arlene. She swore that she had never used anyone, at least not intentionally. But they didn't seem to hear her.

Her stomach muscles twisted small and tried to back away. She was going to start gagging and choking any minute. Fabe and Bobby approached. She thought they would stand up for her. Instead, they slapped her like a volleyball, pushing her back toward the others and swinging round again, laughing like the kids in school. She doubled over. This time she wasn't faking the pain, and no one believed her.

The pain was out of control, and they wouldn't stop. She fought to open her eyes, but they were weighted down. They had tied down her hands. She saw Shelley, Annette, and Paul over by the door, their faces distorted, as if every bone showed through. Pete was moving closer, step by heavy step, one enormous foot clanking down in front of the other, the drum beats she had worked so hard to keep pace with. They were chanting in chorus now, each voice distinct, growing almost louder than the pain: "You used us. Now we'll use you. You used us. Now we'll use you. You used us. You used us. Now we'll make you suffer."

𝄞 "Stop it," she cried out.

"Stop what?" Suddenly Annette's voice was gentle, laughing, making fun of her. No, there was no sarcasm. She opened her eyes and saw Sally sitting there.

"Sorry. I must have been dreaming." She tried to sit up and felt the blood rush to her head.

"Take it easy," Sally said. "We can wait a while."

"You must have other things to do."

"Just take you home, that's all. Relax."

"I guess I have to." It was all she could do to lie back down again. There was no pain, though, just the dizziness.

"She had certainly better relax," a nurse said. "She used up all her strength in that chair." She walked over smiling. "Are you feeling calmer now?"

"I guess so. What do you mean I used up all my strength? What did I do?"

"You tried to stop the doctor, for one thing," she laughed. "I had to slap your arm down, and you were hanging onto his arm like it was life or death."

"I'm sorry."

"A lot of patients get like that, if they feel a little pain, even though they're asleep. You were fighting harder than most of them."

"I have a feeling you're a lot stronger than you think you are," Sally teased.

In another fifteen minutes, she could sit up. Half an hour later, Sally was hailing a cab. An hour later, she was lying in her own bed, while Sally busied herself straightening up the apartment, "making her comfortable," running out to the store for cans of soup in case she got hungry. By three o'clock, after a hundred assurances that she was fine, a hundred promises that she'd call if she needed anything, Sally was gone. They were all gone—Sally, Annette, Shelley, Bob, Pete, Frankie, Fabe, Dick, Paul, Bobby. But Sally was the only one she missed. She was the only one who had really been there.

𝄞 At five o'clock on the dot, her mother called. "I just wanted to be sure you're okay. How are you feeling?"

Her mother's shrill voice jolted her permanently into reality. "I'm fine."

"You didn't call. We were worried."

"I'm fine. I was sleeping, that's all."

"I knew we shouldn't have called. I told Daddy you were probably asleep and we'd waken you. But we were worried."

"No, I'm glad you called." She tried to sound convincing.

"Do you need anything?"

"No."

"I thought we'd drive up tomorrow. Are there any records or anything we can bring you? I'll make a macaroni and cheese casserole tonight. You know how you love that, and it's easy to chew."

"There's no need to come up, really. Sally bought some soup, and I'm really feeling fine. There's hardly any pain, and the gum's not swollen."

"You're putting ice packs on it, aren't you? Are you remembering to do that?" Her father's voice.

"It's not swollen. Honest."

"Well, we'll see tomorrow," her mother said. "Maybe you should come home for a few days. Daddy will drive you back."

"I have to work Monday. There's no need to come up, really. Besides, I already made plans to take in a movie with Sally tomorrow afternoon."

Silence. No, shock. Finally they made her promise to call if she needed anything, to call tomorrow night even if she didn't need anything, so they'd know she was okay. She tried to go back to sleep, but she was feeling restless now.

It wasn't easy for her parents, but they would have to give up all their old fantasies, too. Her mother, especially, would have to make her own friends to fill the empty space. Sooner or later, everyone had to do that, but there was no way they could understand before they were ready.